D0407120

Also by
SARAH DARER LITTMAN

Charmed, I'm Sure

FAIREST OF THEM ALL

Also by
SARAH DARER LITTMAN

Charmed, I'm Sure

FAIREST OF THEM ALL

SARAH DARER LITTMAN

ALADDIN
New York London Toronto Sydney New Delhi

ALADDIN

An imprint of Simon & Schuster Children's Publishing Division

1230 Avenue of the Americas, New York, New York 10020

First Aladdin hardcover edition May 2017

Text copyright © 2017 by Sarah Darer Littman

Jacket illustration copyright © 2017 by Angela Navarra

Also available in an Aladdin paperback edition.

All rights reserved, including the right of reproduction in whole or in part in any form.

ALADDIN and related logo are registered trademarks of Simon & Schuster, Inc.

For information about special discounts for bulk purchases, please contact Simon & Schuster Special Sales at 1-866-506-1949 or business@simonandschuster.com.

The Simon & Schuster Speakers Bureau can bring authors to your live event. For more information or to book an event contact the Simon & Schuster Speakers Bureau at 1-866-248-3049 or visit our website at www.simonspeakers.com.

Book designed by Laura Lyn DiSiena

The text of this book was set in Bembo Infant.

Manufactured in the United States of America 0417 FFG

10 9 8 7 6 5 4 3 2 1

This book has been cataloged with the Library of Congress.

ISBN 978-1-4814-5130-7 (hc)

ISBN 978-1-4814-5129-1 (pbk)

ISBN 978-1-4814-5131-4 (eBook)

For Lindsay Cullingford and Julia Binnie:
**"We've come a long, long way together,
through the hard times, and the good."**
—"Praise You," Fatboy Slim

Chapter One

**New! Love fashion? Want to learn how
to design and make your own clothes?
Come to Couture Club with Ms. Amara—
Thursday after school 3–5 p.m.**

BEING IN MIDDLE SCHOOL IS HARD WHEN
all you've wanted to do is be a fashion designer for as
long as you can remember. It's even harder when that's
your life's goal but you've been banned from even looking
at a needle. Seriously, if you think *you've* got helicopter
parents, try having a mom who fell asleep for a century
at the age of fifteen because she pricked her finger on a
spindle, despite the fact that her dad, the king, had sup-
posedly ordered every one in the land destroyed. Takes
some doing, huh?

You'd think the takeaway would be that no matter how
much you try to protect your kids from everything, you

can't, even if you're the most powerful person in the land.

Stuff happens.

But apparently my parents (you know Mom as Sleeping Beauty, because of her looks and, well, obvious reasons) didn't get the moral of their own story. Instead, they're overprotective freaks who live in constant fear of me encountering anything sharp because it might send me into a lengthy nap.

It puts a serious damper on my life, let me tell you.

"Aria, your life is totally made!" my best friend, Sophie, exclaims, thrusting a bright-yellow handout in my face so enthusiastically that she almost gives me a paper cut on my nose.

"Careful!" I say. "So what exactly is this life-making miracle?"

"You know the new teacher, Ms. Amara?" Sophie says, handing me the paper and sitting down with her lunch. "She's starting a couture club."

I can't believe my ears. But when I look at the handout, it's there in black and yellow:

There's a sketch of a needle and thread, a sewing machine, and a mannequin wearing a supercool dress.

"This is a dream come true!" I exclaim.

"Tell me about it," Sophie says. "I thought of you the minute I saw the poster on the notice board. You should go sign up today."

"I will," I say, imagining all the amazing outfits I'm going to design and make.

Then I look at the handout again and reality hits.

"Uh, actually . . . no. I won't," I say with a sigh, turning the flyer facedown so I don't have to look at it. I slide it back across the cafeteria table, mourning my crushed dreams.

Sophie stares at me like I'm a few sandwiches short of a picnic. "Why not? This club was made for you!"

"I know," I say. "But look"—I turn over the handout and point to the pictures of the sewing machine and the needle—"SHARP OBJECT ALERT. My parents would totally freak."

"But Couture Club is in school," Sophie says. "It's supervised. And educational."

"I know. But that won't matter to Mom and Dad. They're crazy."

"We live in New York City," Sophie points out, like I somehow forgot the place I was born and raised. "Not Fairy Tale Land."

"You assume my parents are rational people."

"They seem rational enough to me," Sophie says.

"They are when it comes to most things," I admit. "But me being near objects that might prick my finger and put me to sleep is not one of them."

"You're lucky you aren't diabetic, like Luca," Sophie mutters. Luca's her little brother. He has to prick his finger before every meal to check his blood sugar, the poor kid.

"I know. Mom's head would literally explode just thinking about it. And I mean *literally*."

"*Ewww.* I'm eating, Aria. Can you *not*?" Sophie complains. Apparently she doesn't appreciate a side of gore with her tuna melt.

"There's got to be a way to figure this out," she continues. "Couture Club is so perfect for you."

"If you can think of a way, tell me, please!" I say. "But there's no way my parents will let me do it. Remember when I wanted to make clothes for Wisteria?"

Wisteria was the American Girl doll my grandparents bought me. The one that was supposed to be my mini me. I didn't like the dress my grandparents bought me to match hers. It was so last century. I knew I could make her an outfit to match *my* clothes, the ones I actually liked. I worked on sketches for weeks and saved my allowance for the material I'd need. But when I finally had enough money and asked Mom if she would take me to the fabric store, she said no, her face suddenly paling as she gripped the kitchen counter for support.

"Why not?" I asked her, barely able to speak through the lump of anger and frustration swelling in my throat. "It's not fair. I've been saving up my allowance."

It seemed like an eternity before she answered, but it wasn't, because I could hear the pendulum of the antique wall clock hanging above the kitchen table going *ticktock, ticktock.* . . .

It was actually nine seconds, because I'd counted.

"It's too . . . risky," Mom finally said.

"Why?" I asked, although even at that age I was pretty sure I knew.

"You remember what happened to me, Aria," Mom said.

"How could I forget? There are, like, *gazillions* of books and movies, not to mention that ginormous castle at the amusement park."

"Dad and I don't want anything like that to happen to you."

"But, Mom, that was a long time ago!" I pointed out. "Things are different now."

She reached out to touch my cheek, but I jerked my face away because I was so mad.

"The world may have changed, but evil remains the

same," she said. "It just hides under a different face."

"Don't you think evil has better things to do than hang out at a fabric store?" I shouted, before stomping off to my room and sulking for the rest of the afternoon. That was the day I vowed that I'm going to be a fashion designer, no matter how much it freaks out my parents.

To try and educate myself, I've watched every episode of *Teen Couture* that's ever aired—but always when my parents are out.

Sophie doesn't remember the Wisteria incident, so I have to remind her. Telling the story makes me mad all over again, and it leaves my friend frowning.

"This is going to take some serious plotting," she says. But then she smiles. "But you know me—I love figuring out a good plot."

I start clearing my lunch from the table. "Fine. Put that plot-tastic brain of yours to work, because I *need* to do this," I tell her.

"I'm on it," Sophie says, taking all her garbage to throw away. "I'll have this figured out by the end of the day. Trust me."

I don't even have to wait till the end of the day. Sophie's got a plan figured out by sixth-period social studies.

"Chess!" she says triumphantly the minute she sees me.
"What about it?"

"You tell your parents you're joining the Chess Club.
They can't object to that. Even the pointiest chess piece
couldn't prick your finger and send you into la-la land."

Life hack: Be sure to pick a bestie who is both smart
and good at scheming.

"Did I ever tell you what a genius you are?" I say.

"Possibly," Sophie says. "But feel free to repeat it. It
can't be said enough."

"Don't get too carried away," I say. "But I have to
admit, it is a brilliant plan. How can Mom and Dad
object to me wanting to play a game that involves kings,
queens, and knights? It's *so* up their alley."

"There you go!" Sophie exclaims. "Problem solved."

Mr. Falcone starts class, so we can't talk anymore, but
by the time class is over, I've designed two fab outfits in
the margin of my notebook.

Couture Club, here I come!

Mom brings home leftovers for dinner from a fancy
luncheon her company catered at the Pierre. My mother
runs one of New York City's most exclusive party
planning businesses, Enchanted Soirées—tagline: *No*

one slumbers at our *exciting, elegant parties!* She decided on party planning as a vocation because it was my grandpa Thibault's failure at it that caused her century-long sleep.

When Mom was born, my grandparents threw this big shindig to celebrate, inviting anyone who was anyone. There were thirteen wisewomen in the kingdom, but Grandma and Grandpa had only twelve gold plates. Instead of doing the smart thing, namely going down to the Once Upon a Time equivalent of Bed Bath & Beyond and picking up an extra place setting, Gramps decided to leave one of the wisewomen off the guest list. We all know how well *that* went down. Pro tip: Don't ever mess with a wisewoman with FOMO.

My mother decided her life's mission is to make sure no other boneheaded head of household makes a similar mistake just to save a few bucks.

At any rate, it means we get really good leftovers from all these posh parties, which is good because Mom works so hard she's usually too tired to cook. Meanwhile Dad handles the entertainment side of things. His specialty is creating spectacle. I guess once you've watched the thicket of thorns that killed lesser princes melt away before your shining sword, thrilling a few hundred people at bar mitzvahs and weddings is no biggie.

Apparently the ladies who lunched at the Pierre were very impressed with the string quartet Dad had rustled up. According to Mom, they were even more impressed with Dad.

"You should have seen them, Aria," she tells me as she passes the pine-nut-and-lemon orzo. "When Dad arrived all princed-up in uniform and started kissing hands, I thought I was going to have to call 911."

Dad laughs. "You better watch your back, Rose. That nice old dear with the fancy hat and the oxygen tank pinched my behind when you weren't looking."

"*Ewwww.* Dad!" I groan. "I'm eating dinner!"

My parents exchange a glance and start laughing, like making me nauseous is the most amusing thing ever. And they're supposed to be the mature ones.

I need to change the subject. Fast.

"So I'm thinking of joining the Chess Club," I announce casually. "I need another extracurricular."

Just as I thought, Dad is all over it. Parents are so predictable. "That's a great idea!" he exclaims. "A princess of royal blood needs to learn strategic thinking, inductive reasoning, and most of all, how to control her knights and pawns."

"Yeah. Right. That's exactly what I had in mind," I lie.

Mom, however, is gazing at me with a furrowed brow marking her face, which is otherwise unlined thanks to some expensive face cream she gets from her favorite website, CharmingLifestyles.com.

"You've always been bored silly by chess, Aria," she says. "Why the sudden interest?"

She knows me well enough to be suspicious. It's annoying, but in a way, I kind of respect her for it.

"Because I want to do well in school so I can be successful, and my math teacher said chess helps your brain work better."

Dad looks like he's about to explode with pride.

"What do you think of our girl, Rose?" he says, beaming. "She's the brightest leaf on the family tree, this one."

"Yes, she's definitely bright," Mom says. "But this still seems . . . odd."

"Well, I think it's great," Dad says. "I can't wait to challenge you to a chess match, Aria."

Yikes. Talk about a snag in our cunning plan. I never thought about the fact that Dad might actually want to play chess with me. This means I'm going to really have to *learn how to play chess*, something I have absolutely zero interest in doing. *Ugh.*

"Yay! Can't wait," I say, summoning as much false enthusiasm as I can. "It'll be so much fun."

But not nearly as much fun as what I'm *really* going to be doing instead of chess—designing and making my own clothes at Couture Club.

Chapter Two

I'M FIDGETING IN MY SEAT AND COUNTING down the minutes till the final bell rings, because today is the first meeting of Couture Club. My notebook margins are filled with ideas for outfits I want to make. I can't wait to throw myself into a room full of scissors and needles and, who knows, maybe even a *sewing machine*! Living on the edge, that's me.

What Mom and Dad don't know won't hurt them.

Earlier this week, I asked Alex Lobachevsky, who really *is* a member of the Chess Club, if he could give me some pointers on how to learn the basics of chess in a hurry. He looked at me as if I'd asked him to poison his kitten.

"Chess isn't something you can learn in a hurry," he sniffed. "Not if you want to play well."

"I don't need to play well," I said. "Just . . . enough to fake it."

This moved me to an even lower status in his eyes, something I didn't think was possible.

With a long-suffering sigh, he gave me the names of some online chess tutorials. When I watched them in my room with headphones on so my parents couldn't hear, it was clear they were meant for kids in kindergarten, which is apparently where Alex thinks I belong if I only want to play chess to squeak by. Whatever. Chess is *his* passion. For me, it's just a smoke screen so I can be free to do mine.

When school's finally over, I leap out of my seat, grab my stuff, and give Sophie a high five.

"Have fun!" she says. "And beware of anything pointy!"

I give her a stink eye. "Don't. Even. Joke."

"You'll be fine," Sophie says. "This isn't a fairy story. We have science."

"Tell that to my parents," I grumble as I head out of the room toward my destiny.

There are already eight other students in Ms. Amara's classroom when I get there. I know most of them, but

there are two new kids I've only seen around school—
twins who moved here from Canada at the beginning of
the year. Dakota, the boy, always wears a wool beanie,
but I hear him telling Matt Landers that it's called a
tuque. I guess that's Canadian for "beanie." His twin sister's name is Nina. She's sitting quietly by herself while
everyone else is talking. She looks kind of lonely, so I take
a seat next to her and introduce myself.

"Hey, Nina, I'm Aria Thornbrier. How do you like it
at Manhattan World Themes Middle School so far?"

"It's okay," she says, shrugging her slim shoulders. "It's
just really . . . different here. Everything in New York is
so . . . loud and crowded. And fast."

"Where did you live before?" I ask her. "I mean, I
know you're from Canada, but where?"

"Out west," Nina says. "We grew up in the forests of
British Columbia. But when Dad married our stepmother
last summer, our aunt Gretel insisted we move to New
York to live with her." She fidgets with a gold bracelet of
small leaf-shaped links that she's wearing on her delicate
wrist. "I'd never been to a city before we came to live
here," she admits.

"Never? Like, you mean as in never ever?"

"Never ever. Not once."

I try to imagine coming to live in Manhattan if you've never even been in a city before. I can't.

"Wow. Talk about culture shock," I say.

"Tell me about it. I don't remember what it feels like to sleep a whole night," she says with a sigh. "It's so *noisy*. Even at night, I can still hear cars honking. Don't even get me started on those stupid sirens, which hurt my brain. I've tried earplugs and burying my head under pillows, but . . ."

"You'll get used to it eventually," I assure her. "I hardly ever notice street noise anymore."

"I hope you're right," she says. "I miss hearing the call of the spotted owl instead of the constant buzz of traffic."

It's funny because when we've visited friends outside the city, I've found it just as hard to sleep because it's so *quiet*. When it's that quiet, every little sound you *do* hear seems magnified, and you scream and wake up half the house because you're convinced it's a ghost or a burglar instead of your friend's stupid cat jumping off her bed onto the wood floor.

Not that this ever happened to me, of course. I'm speaking *hypothetically*.

Ms. Amara walks in carrying a coffee in a travel mug that says: I'M A TEACHER. WHAT'S YOUR SUPERPOWER?

I like her already. Her outfit is impressive: a floaty-sleeve Indian-print tunic with these cool little mirrors sewn into it, with dark leggings and a styling pair of wedge heels. Her maroon lipstick is perfectly applied, something I haven't yet managed, despite lots of experimenting with Mom's makeup while she's out being the Queen of Enchanted Soirées.

She puts her coffee down on the desk and surveys us all, wearing a big smile.

"Who's ready to create some fabulous fashion?" she asks.

We all just look around at one another. No one's willing to be the first to be fabulous—until Nina raises her hand.

"Yes! Good!" Ms. Amara exclaims. "Nina, isn't it?"

My new friend nods and says yes so quietly, I can barely hear her.

But her quiet courage inspires me to raise my hand.

"Great! We have another fashion enthusiast! And you are . . . ?"

"Aria," I tell her.

"Wonderful!" Ms. Amara exclaims.

Her enthusiasm is so contagious that soon everyone is admitting their desire to be fabulous—or at least that they want to learn how to design and make cool outfits.

"Every designer starts with a vision," Ms. Amara

says. "And to help you with that, we're going to create mood boards."

"Wait—is this earthy, crunchy New Age psychology stuff?" Matt complains. "'Cause I just want to make clothes."

Ms. Amara laughs. "It isn't about *your* mood so much as the colors and inspirations for your collection," she explains. "Although of course that may well reflect the mood of the designer or the times. You should each take a piece of poster board, a pair of scissors, and a stack of magazines—plus any little fabric remnants that strike your fancy. Cut out photographs that inspire you, colors, quotes, people whose style you admire."

"Oh, okay. Now I get it," Matt says, obviously relieved. "That's cool."

I go up to get poster board and scissors. Nina grabs a stack of magazines and glue for the both of us. Then we rummage through a plastic crate of fabric scraps that Ms. Amara has behind her desk. Dakota grabs a scrap of silk camo fabric that looks like trees in a wood.

"You can take the boy out of the woods, but you can't take the woods out of the boy," Nina jokes.

"Like you're one to talk," Dakota says, looking at the mossy-green velvet scrap she has in her hand.

"Busted," I say, smiling at both of them.

"Dakota, this is Aria," Nina says. "She says I'll get used to the street noise eventually."

"I hope so," Dakota says. "Nina keeps waking me up complaining that she can't sleep," he tells me. "I mean, what am *I* supposed to do about it?"

"You're my twin!" Nina says. "You're supposed to sense my feelings and stuff."

"That's hocus-pocus, not science," Dakota says. "Just read a book or go get a drink of milk or something, and let me sleep, okay?"

There are plenty of times I've wished I weren't an only child. Now is not one of them.

Dakota and Matt come to sit at the same table, and we have a great time comparing pictures we're cutting out for our boards. I manage to wield a pair of sharp scissors without any damage to myself or anyone around me, which goes to show that my parents are way overprotective and need therapy to work out the trauma of their past before they mess me up, too.

My mood board has pictures of famous people like Beyoncé, Natalie Portman, and Reese Witherspoon wearing purple dresses; pieces of purple, silver, and white fabric; and a scrap of turquoise lace I found at the bottom of Ms. Amara's crate. I've also pasted a quote that's attributed to Eleanor Roosevelt: "The future belongs to those who believe in the beauty of their dreams."

"What's with all the purple?" Dakota asks. "Do you have royal aspirations or something?"

I hesitate, wondering if I should tell him that I don't need to aspire—that I'm a Princess of the Blood Royal, something my parents and grandparents remind me of every time I don't stand up straight or don't dress well or use a bad word. But being Sleeping Beauty's daughter comes with a lot of baggage—especially in a situation where there are sharp things everywhere.

I decide to keep mum for now.

"No, purple's my favorite color, that's all."

But then I wonder *why* it's my favorite color. Is it in my royal DNA or something?

My parents and grandparents always give me a hard time because I just want to be a normal kid. "Why try to pretend you aren't a princess?" Dad asks constantly. "Be proud of who you are."

"Can't I be a princess and normal at the same time?" I ask him.

"Not if your mother is anything to go by" is his favorite quip.

Rim shot.

But even though he jokes about Mom, he couldn't be more proud of the way she turned a bad experience into a positive, using Grandpa Thibault's party-planning faux pas as a springboard to create a successful business.

When we've finished our mood boards, Ms. Amara tells us to sketch some pieces that the board inspires.

"Then next week we'll create a pattern and start transforming your design into couture," she says.

As the sketch of a purple skirt takes shape under my pencil, excitement blossoms within me like the roses on the thorny briars surrounding the castle where Mom took her one-hundred-year nap.

"I can't wait till next week," Nina says. "When we get to make the ideas we've drawn on paper come to life."

"I know," I say. "But I'm even more excited for when we finally get to wear them!"

Chapter Three

"HOW ABOUT A NICE GAME OF CHESS?"
Dad asks me on Sunday morning. "Do you think Chess
Club has prepared you to beat Prince Daddy-O yet?"

I've been trying to force myself to do one chess tutorial
a day, just in case of this eventuality, but there's no way
I'm ready to play Prince Daddy-O, much less beat him.

"Um . . . not today," I say. "I've got too much
homework."

This isn't any truer than me going to Chess Club. I
mean, I *do* have homework, but not so much that I couldn't
spend an hour playing a game with my dad. If it were
any other game than chess, I'd be fine with it: Scrabble,

Monopoly, gin rummy. Anything but chess—because if we play that, he'll see that I'm just as bad at it as I was before, and wonder why.

So I end up piling on one lie to cover up the other. "Oh, what a tangled web we weave, when first we practice to deceive!" That's what Sir Walter Scott says—or, more accurately, said. He's one of those long-dead poets who summed things up well.

But I can't help noticing the disappointed look my tangled web of deception leaves on Dad's face. He and Mom were out late working this fancy gala at the Metropolitan Museum of Art last night. It was one of Enchanted Soirées' biggest parties of the year—they've been planning it practically since the day after the last one finished.

Following a night of heavy prince duties, Dad likes his family time. So I slump onto the sofa next to him, careful not to disturb our fourteen-year-old corgi, Mozart.

"How did it go last night?" I ask.

"Without a hitch," Dad says with a proud smile. "Your mom's the best in the business."

"Did you bedazzle them with your princely splendor?" Dad laughs.

"Oh yeah," he says. "A royal uniform, a chest full of medals, and a ceremonial sword—nothing like it to

set the hearts of Manhattan socialites aflutter."

"But you don't want to set them aflutter, for reals?" I ask, stroking Mozart's ear and carefully avoiding looking Dad in the eye. "You and Mom are always going to live happily ever after, right?"

"Of course we are, Aria," Dad says. I meet his eyes and he looks puzzled. "How could you think otherwise? You know the prince thing is just my party trick to help business. I do it because Enchanted Soirées is important to Rose, and you and Rose are the most important people in the world to me."

"Yeah. I know," I mumble. Mozart raises his head and puts his graying muzzle on my knee.

"So what's all this about, then?" Dad asks.

"Nothing really," I say. "It's just . . . we've got these new kids in school. Twins. They moved here from western Canada, some place in the boonies. They have to live with their aunt because their dad got remarried, and it's hard 'cause they're used to living in the woods."

"From the backwoods of Canada to the middle of Manhattan? I can see how that would be a pretty big culture shock," Dad says. "It took your mom and me a while to get used to living here too. But Grandpa Thibault probably had the hardest adjustment of all."

"Why him?"

Dad laughs.

"Well . . . let's just say that it took him a while to get used to the concept of *democracy*," he says. "When you're used to ruling your own kingdom and then a New York cabbie starts telling you where to go because you didn't give him a big enough tip—"

"*Ohmigosh,* I can't *imagine* what Grandpa would do!"

"I'll tell you what happened," Dad says. "First Grandma Althea hit the poor cabbie with her handbag while asking him if he knew he was addressing THE KING, then Grandpa Thibault threatened to have him flogged for insolence."

It's totally wrong of me to laugh at the thought of my grandparents threatening violence to a New York cabbie, but it's like a scene from a really bad comedy starring my relatives.

"Oh no . . . they didn't."

"Oh yes . . . they did," Dad continues. "Then the cabbie called Grandpa a sicko and called the police. Mom and I had to bail the pair of them out of the Thirteenth Precinct."

"Wait. You had to bail Grandma and Grandpa *out of jail?*"

"We did indeed. When Mom and I got there, Grandpa was shouting about how poor the conditions were, compared to the dungeons in his castle, and did they know who they were dealing with?"

"What about Grandma?"

"She was going on about how the mayor would hear about it and they would all lose their badges."

My grandparents, the ex-cons. *Who knew?*

"You think Mom and I embarrass you, Aria? You've got it made in the shade compared to what we've had to put up with."

"Maybe. Just don't ever say 'made in the shade' in public, okay?"

"Okay. I will put it in the Uncool Folder," Dad says, taking my hand. "Listen, sweetheart. Don't ever worry about your mom and me. We plan to live out our fairy-tale ending, right to the very end, okay?" He gives my hand a reassuring squeeze and smiles. "Do you want some pancakes?"

How can I say no to that? We end up watching *The Princess Bride* for what must be the three hundred eighty-seventh time. But I don't care. It's one of my favorite movies, and at least I get out of playing chess.

❋

On Tuesday after school, Nina and I head to Sew Many Options in the Garment District to buy fabric for our project. Ms. Amara helped us estimate roughly how much we'd need. Good thing I have some allowance saved up so I don't have to ask Mom and Dad for money. Sophie tags along, even though she's more into coding than couture.

The store is long and narrow, and shelves go from floor to ceiling, holding bolts of fabric. I don't even know how we're supposed to see stuff, much less choose. An older lady, who is barely five feet tall, with white hair and cat-eye glasses perched on the top of her head, asks, "Do you young ladies need any help?"

"We're looking for fabric," Nina says.

The lady gestures to the wall-to-wall shelves of the stuff. "Looks like you came to the right place."

She says it with a wry smile, but Nina obviously isn't used to dry humor. She starts flushing and looks upset, like she thinks the lady dissed her. I jump in to smooth things over.

"We're in the Couture Club at school. I've designed this skirt. . . ." I whip out my cell and show her a picture I took of my sketch.

"Hold on, I need my glasses to look at that," the lady says. "The perils of old age."

She goes back to the register desk and starts shuffling papers around.

"Um . . . I think your glasses are on your head," I remind her.

She reaches her hand up and touches them.

"Why, so they are! Thank you!"

After placing the readers on the end of her nose, she comes back over and leans in close to look at my skirt.

"I wanted to get purple fabric for the skirt, with a turquoise lining. What do you recommend?"

"Interesting design," she says. "And I love the contrast lining and lace detail. Bold choice of colors. You've got an eye, young lady."

I feel a warm flush of pride. "Thanks," I mumble. She must see a lot of people come in here looking for fabric, so her compliment means a lot.

"Let me see. . . . My suggestions would be a poly cotton or, if you want something more autumnal, a wool blend. And for the lining, maybe a silk charmeuse or a Bemberg rayon."

She leads me down the long row. "Poly cottons are up here on your right. Wool blends are on the lower two shelves on your left, on the next set of shelves. Silks are farther down on the right."

I start going through the wool blends while Nina explains that she's making a shift dress and wants something green and natural that reminds her of trees, because she misses the forests of Canada where she grew up.

"Chiffon for you," the lady says. She tells us her name is Mrs. Wildvogel. "That means 'wild bird' in German, Miss Forest Girl. And let me tell you, I was a wild bird in my day."

"Hard to believe now," Sophie whispers to me.

But I disagree. She might have white hair and liver spots on her wrinkled hands, but her brown eyes dance in a way I bet she wishes her feet still could.

I find purple-and-black jacquard wool that's perfect for my skirt. I can see myself in it now, with a pair of black tights and cool boots. Then I search out the silk charmeuse. It's more expensive, so I decide to go with the Bemberg rayon.

"What do you think of this?" Nina calls out. She shows us green chiffon with a pattern of tiny leaves.

"That's so you," Sophie says.

"Definitely. It has Forest Girl written all over it," I tell her.

Mrs. Wildvogel approves of our choices and helps us with yardage and notions. She even gives us a student discount for showing our school IDs.

"Come back to show me your finished garments," she says.

We promise to do that, and also to tell the rest of Couture Club about the student discount.

Before taking the bus back to the East Side, we stop in at a nearby coffee shop for a snack. After we sit down, I start trying to stuff my fabric bag into my backpack.

There's no way it'll all fit in the backpack with my books.

"What am I going to do?" I ask Sophie. "Walking into the apartment with a bag from Sew Many Options would totally blow my cover."

Nina looks confused.

"What do you mean, blow your cover?" she asks.

"You don't know about Aria's parents?" Sophie says.

"No," Nina says. "What about them?"

"Aria, I think you should take it from here," Sophie says.

So I have to tell Nina that I'm Sleeping Beauty's daughter, and how because of that, my parents are . . . well, the way they are. So I've had to come up with a cover story to attend Couture Club.

"And that's why I can't walk in with a bag from a fabric store. Because then they'll know I lied."

"I can take your fabric home and bring it on Thursday," Nina says. "That way, you don't have to worry about it."

"Are you sure?" I ask. "That would be awesome!"

"No problem!" she says.

"A problem shared is a problem solved," Sophie says.

She's right. Maybe I should do it more often.

It's like a more fashionable version of show-and-tell at the beginning of Couture Club as we let everyone else see the fabrics we picked out for our projects. But Ms. Amara doesn't let us sit around for too long.

"We don't have a lot of time to get these made, so start cutting. But don't rush it. Be careful. Slow and steady wins the race."

It's hard to be patient and do every step slowly, because I want to see my sketch as a real garment—and more importantly, *wear* it. But Ms. Amara keeps reminding us, "As you sew, so you shall rip." She says that we have to take the time to get it right so that what we make lasts.

I have other considerations: If I rush things, there's a higher risk of pricking my finger. It's not like I actually *believe* my parents' mumbo jumbo about needle danger. I'm a Modern Twenty-First-Century Girl. I'm all about critical thinking and science, things that can be proven. Spells and enchantments? They're the stuff of the old tales from Once Upon a Time. But still . . . better safe than sorry, right?

I manage to pin the pattern to the fabric with oh-so-sharp pins and cut it with those super-dangerous scissors without doing myself any deathly injuries. I am woman, watch me slice and dice!

Even when I use the sewing machine to sew seams of the lining and the skirt, it goes off without a hitch or a scratch. My future as a fashion designer is looking brighter by the minute.

I'm sewing one of the fasteners on by hand when I accidentally prick myself with the needle.

"Ow!" I exclaim, and look in horror as a dot of dark-red blood wells from the pad of my thumb. Some of it drips onto the purple-and-black fabric. "No!"

"What's the matter?" Nina asks.

"I pricked my finger," I tell her. "Okay, this is going to sound totally weird, but . . . if I suddenly fall asleep, can you call my parents?"

"Why would you suddenly— Oh," Nina says, remembering our conversation from the other day and realizing why a thumb prick might equal sudden sleepiness.

"I mean, I'm sure nothing will happen," I say, hoping she doesn't notice the wobble of uncertainty in my voice.

"That stuff all happened Once Upon a Time. This is just a regular needle. Nothing enchanted about it."

I'm not sure if I'm trying to reassure Nina or myself.

"Of course!" she agrees, but her brow is furrowed and I see her quickly glance at the wall clock and back at me, as if she's counting down the seconds it might take for me to collapse into sleep for the next century.

We both stare at the drop of blood on my thumb. I feel my heart beating faster than the second hand on the clock. What if my parents were right? Looking on the bright side, at least I'll be asleep, so I won't have to hear them say, "We told you so."

After a minute, Nina asks, "Are you feeling sleepy?"

She sounds like Kaa from *The Jungle Book*.

"No, so far so good."

After two minutes go by and I'm still wide awake, we look at each other and start laughing.

"Not even a teensy-weensy bit tired?" Nina asks.

"Nope. If anything, I'm hyper!"

To prove it, I get up and dance over to the sink to wash the blood off my thumb.

"What got into you?" Matt asks.

"I'm just happy, that's all," I say. "And AWAKE!"

Matt glances over at Dakota, who is sewing a

seam on his urban-camouflage tuxedo vest.

"Dakota, Aria says she's happy because she's awake at four thirty in the afternoon. Do we have an official ruling that girls are weird?"

Ms. Amara, who overhears Matt as she walks back to her desk, lifts her travel mug of coffee. "If it weren't for coffee, I'm not sure *I'd* be awake at four thirty in the afternoon," she says, winking at me. "There's nothing weird about that."

"Matt, looks like you've been served." Dakota grins.

"Whatever. It's almost time to clean up anyway."

I quickly finish sewing the fastener onto my skirt before I clean up, because I want to wear it home. The hem is still only tacked, but I'll finish that properly next week.

Nina and I clean up our stuff, and I ask her to wait for me while I go change into my skirt in the bathroom.

"Sure," she says. "Maybe we can go for a hot chocolate or something afterward."

I wish we had a full-length mirror in the girls' bathroom so I could see how I look in the skirt. For a minute, I consider standing on the toilet so I can see myself in the mirror above the sink, but knowing my luck, I'd end up with my foot in the toilet, and that would be totally gross and hard to explain to the others. So I have to go on how

I feel, and how I feel is *awesome*—which is how a good outfit is supposed to make you feel, right?

Nina, Dakota, and Matt are waiting for me outside the bathroom door.

"So, where are we heading?" Dakota asks.

"How about Starcups?" I say. "It's the place to go."

Matt gives me a skeptical look. He's MWTMS's self-styled Mr. Trendy New York Hot Spots. It gets kind of annoying sometimes.

"Well, for coffee and hot chocolate, at least," I add.

"It's close and it's the place where kids from our school go," Matt says. "Other than that, it's overpriced and drearily generic."

Like I said, annoying.

"Starcups it is," Dakota says. "Lead the way."

I love how my new skirt swishes around my legs as I walk down the street. I might have to get a new pair of boots to go with it, if and when my allowance ever gets to the level where I can afford new boots.

"What are you going to tell your parents?" Nina says.

"What do you mean?" I ask.

"About the outfit," she says. "When they ask you where you got it."

Great. Another lie I have to come up with. They keep

piling up like yellow snow on the street corner after a
blizzard.

"Good question. And I have no answer yet."

"You could tell them I made it for you," Nina says.

"You're going to help Aria lie?" Dakota says.

"What's it to you?" Nina asks, raising her chin.

"Nothing," Dakota says. "It's just . . . not like you."

I don't want to be a bad influence. It's bad enough *I'm*
turning into such a deceitful daughter without corrupting
Nina with my lying ways.

"You don't have to," I tell her.

"I know I don't," she says. "But I want to, because you're
my friend. One of the only friends I've got in this city."

"If you're sure," I say. "It would give me an out with
Mom and Dad."

"Will she or won't she? That is the question." Matt puts
on a fake British accent, like he's narrating a PBS docu-
mentary. "Will this rare species from the remote woods of
Canada, rarely seen in Manhattan's noisy streets, adapt
to the duplicitous ways of city life?"

"Ohmigosh, you guys," Nina says, laughing, as we
walk into Starcups. "Why are you making such a big
deal? It's fine."

We order our drinks from the barista, who is dressed

in black from top to toe and looks like her mood is that way too. I wonder if she's having a bad day.

"We'll go nab some seats," Matt says.

"Yeah, there are some over by the window," Dakota tells us as he heads off to hunt for empty chairs.

Nina watches her brother walk away.

"I wish he'd stop acting like he's my dad," she says. "Because he's not. He's my twin brother. And I'm three minutes and forty-two seconds older than he is, so he has no right to boss me around."

"Yeah, I know. My parents are totally overprotective," I say sympathetically. "It's super annoying. But maybe he's just concerned?"

"I guess," she admits. "Sometimes I wish he'd worry a little less so I could just be myself."

"Excuse me. . . ."

We turn and see a tall, striking woman behind us, dressed in an elegant black pantsuit. I can't help but notice how ace her accessories are. Fab shoes, a great bag, and really amazing signature jewelry pieces on her ears, neck, and wrists. She knows what she's doing, fashion-wise, that's for sure.

"I just *love* your skirt," she tells me. "Where did you get it?"

I'm flooded with pride and paralyzed with amazement that someone other than my parents likes something I created, especially someone who is really well dressed and doesn't even know me.

"She made it," Nina says before I can get my lips moving.

"Really?" the woman says. "Fascinating."

Eyeing me thoughtfully, she reaches into her bag and rummages around while Nina and I pick up our drinks.

"I'm Adele Bonrever," the lady says, holding out a card in her immaculately manicured fingers. "A talent spotter for *Teen Couture*."

I have to bite my cheek to stifle a scream of excitement, because that would be totally dorky and not at all New York. Instead I try to act like this kind of thing happens to me every day—which it doesn't, not even in my wildest dreams.

I take the card and Nina looks at it over my shoulder. It reads: ADELE M. BONREVER. CASTING DIRECTOR. INYOURDREAMS ENTERTAINMENT.

"You want Aria to be on your show?" Nina squeaks.

I hold my breath, waiting for her answer.

"I'd like her to come for a screen test, yes," Ms. Bonrever says.

The barista calls out a small, skinny vanilla latte.

"That's me," Ms. Bonrever says. "How about we sit down and I tell you more about the show?"

We join Matt and Dakota. When Matt hears who Adele is, he jumps up and nearly falls over himself to pull over an extra chair.

"I read that you're casting the new season of *Teen Couture* on tvgossipscoopz.com!" he exclaims.

"I am indeed," Ms. Bonrever says, smiling at him.

Matt's a native New Yorker like me. We're supposed to be immune to celebrity gawking because we see famous people all the time on the streets. I mean I *live* with two of the most famous people of all time. But right now Matt's fanboying worse than someone from the suburbs of Nowheresville. I think the combination of fashion and potential fame has gone to his head.

"As you may know, *Teen Couture* is a show where tweens compete in a series of challenges to make the best outfits. The grand prize for the upcoming season is a week shadowing the scorching-hot designer Seiyariyashi Tomaki in his studio"—Ms. Bonrever pauses as Matt lets out an audible gasp of excitement—"*and* a one-on-one lunch with him where you can ask any questions you have about the industry."

Okay, Matt's not the only one freaking out now. This is a chance of a lifetime. I'm better at keeping a poker face than he is, though. My parents are the best actors I know, but I'm no slouch, either. Years of having to sit through deathly boring parties with Really Important People (RIPs), while still being super polite and pretending you're having a good time, have finally paid off.

"Could be an interesting opportunity," I say with what I hope is cool nonchalance.

"It's an *amazing* opportunity," Ms. Bonrever states. "Tomaki is an unparalleled genius. To get a one-on-one with him before one's career even starts is a gift of incalculable value. But only the winner gets that prize."

I want that prize. I want it more than anything I've ever wanted before in my entire life.

"So, Aria, will you come for a screen test?" Ms. Bonrever asks.

Out of the corner of my eye I see Matt visibly deflate. I feel bad for him, but not bad enough to give up my chance at the prize. All's fair in love and fashion.

"Sure, okay," I say. "Why not?"

Her crimson-painted lips part in a wide smile.

"Wonderful! I think you'll be a terrific fit, and my instincts are rarely wrong," she says, opening her capacious bag again and pulling out a sheet of paper. "I just need your parents to sign this consent form and return it to my office. Scan and e-mail is fine. Then we can set up a time for the screen test."

My vision of picking Seiyariyashi Tomaki's brain about everything I ever wanted to know about the fashion industry over lunch at one of New York's finest restaurants fades to black as soon as I hear the words "consent form."

Because given that these challenges are going to involve needles, pins, and other sharp objects of potentially finger-pricking nature, the chances of my parents signing a consent form range from zero to "not in a million years."

But as I take the form from Adele Bonrever, my smile doesn't waver. Seriously, it's a totally Oscar-worthy performance. No lie. But this is the last of my truths. Because I have to figure out how to take part in *Teen Couture*. And somehow, I have a feeling that's going to involve a *lot* of lying.

Chapter Four

SOPHIE AND NINA ARE UNITED IN THE opinion that I have to find a way to do the screen test— even if it involves subterfuge. Even Matt, who is still totally jealous that Adele Bonrever picked me instead of him, agrees.

"At least if you're on the show, I can live vicariously in your reflected glory," he says. "And you can convince them they should pick me for next season."

"First I actually have to get on the show," I tell him. "I mean, it's easy for you, Soph. You can be honest with your parents, because they're not crazy protective like mine."

"True," she agrees. "But that just leaves me with energy to come up with creative ideas to deceive *your* parents."

"So what's the plan?" Nina asks. "Because I can't think of anything. Forgery isn't my strong point."

"Besides, it's bad enough you've started lying since you came to New York," Dakota says. "You don't need to turn into even more of a delinquent."

Nina rolls her eyes. "Okay, Dad."

"Who are you calling delinquents?" Sophie says. "We're *creatives*."

Dakota snorts, but we choose to ignore his backwoods cynicism.

"Your parents already think you're in the Chess Club, right?" Matt asks.

"Yeah," I confirm. "That was Lie—excuse me, *Creative Explanation*—Number One."

"Don't they have a field trip coming up to the regional heats of the International Chess Federation Tournament?" Matt says. "I heard Alex and Sundar talking about it in math class."

"That's it!" Sophie exclaims. "We'll get a permission slip for the chess field trip, then photocopy it on top of the consent form for *Teen Couture*. Then all you have to do is get one of your parents to sign it when they're doing something else. Parents will sign any old school form when they're distracted."

"That's brilliant," I say. "It could actually work."

"Of course it could work!" Sophie says. "You think I'd propose a plan doomed to fail?"

"No," Dakota says. "You're beginning to terrify me with your evil genius."

"It's not evil, exactly," Nina argues. "More like creatively cunning."

"I like the way you think," Sophie tells her with a smile.

Dakota frowns. I'm pretty sure he thinks Sophie, Matt, and I are bad influences. Hopefully he'll realize we're not once he gets to know us better.

I approach Alex Lobachevsky after school and ask him if he can get me a field trip permission slip.

"Why do you want it?" he asks. "You're not in the Chess Club. You're not even interested in learning to play chess well. Only 'enough to fake it.'"

He does air quotes to emphasize my lameness.

"I have my reasons," I say.

Apparently vague, unspecified "reasons" aren't good enough for Alex.

"Ten dollars," he says.

"What?"

"I'll get you the permission slip for ten dollars."

"You're going to charge me for a permission slip?"

"This is the situation," he says, pinning me with a sharp gaze from behind his black-rimmed glasses. "You need this permission slip for 'reasons,' which it's obvious have nothing to do with going on the field trip. That means this paper has value to you. I will provide the paper to you as a service for compensation. It's called capitalism."

"As American as apple pie, right?"

"Even more American than apple pie," Alex says. "Now, do you want the permission form or not?"

I don't just want it. I *need* it. Desperately. The problem is, I don't have ten dollars to hand over.

"How about five dollars?" I say, holding out the crumpled bills that I do have. "That's all I have on me."

Alex hesitates, then decides that five dollars in hand is better than nothing.

"Ms. Thornbrier, you have yourself a deal," he says, pulling a blank form out of his backpack.

"You had it all along?" I ask, outraged, grabbing it before he changes his mind.

"It's mine. I'll tell Mr. Jackson I lost it and I need another," Alex says, grinning over his shoulder at me as he walks away. "Good luck with your subterfuge, whatever it is."

Alex is probably going to be the head of a big corporation someday.

But instead of being mad, I decide to look at the five dollars I just paid him as an investment in my future. The power of positive thinking and all that.

With both the Chess Club permission form and the *Teen Couture* consent form in hand, I head over to the office-supply place two blocks away, and using one of the glue sticks in the copier area, I glue the top of the Chess Club paper to the bottom of the consent form. After photocopying it to make it look like a single sheet, I cut out the bottom of that sheet and lightly glue it to the real consent form, so that just the signature area shows. That way I can get Mom to sign the real paper, and then just take off the fake sheet and fill in the rest.

I text a picture to Sophie: **What do you think?**

Looks good! She texts back a thumbs-up emoticon. **Catch her when she's distracted.**

I thumbs-up her back and head home. I know Mom doesn't have a party tonight, so there's a good chance she'll be working at her home office. She tries to do that on the nights there isn't an event so she can spend more quality time with me—even if quality time means she's trouble-shooting for an upcoming soirée on her laptop or phone.

Sure enough, when I get home, Mom's there, but she's at the kitchen table with her cell phone glued to her ear and her laptop open in front of her.

"Can you hold on a sec, Snow?" she says. "Aria just walked in."

"Hi, Mom," I say, dumping my backpack. "Are you going to be long?"

"I might be," she says. "I'm on the phone with Rosie White Charming's mom. She's doing a feature piece on Enchanted Soirées for the front page of CharmingLifestyles.com."

"Cool!" I say. "I won't hold you up while you're making money to pay for my glam life." I take the form out of my bag. "I just need you to sign this permission slip for a Chess Club field trip, okay?"

"No problem, honey," Mom says, unmuting the call with Mrs. White Charming. "Hey, Snow, thanks for holding. Yes, we've been selected to do some of the most prestigious fund-raisers this year. Honestly, I think it's because they like having Bernhard show up in his dress uniform. He adds cachet."

I slide the form under her hand as she laughs at whatever Rosie's mom replies.

"I know having their picture taken with a handsome prince seems to encourage people to write bigger checks. Bernhard says he's doing his bit for charity."

She scribbles her signature and continues the conversation as I exhale slowly and carefully take the paper away.

"Thanks!" I whisper, then grab my stuff and make a beeline for my bedroom.

Mission accomplished! ☺ I text Sophie and Nina.

After carefully removing the Chess Club top sheet, I fill in the rest of the consent form, take a picture of it, and e-mail it to Adele Bonrever. I tell her I'm excited to have the opportunity to try out for the show and look forward to hearing from her. I make sure to put my cell-phone number, and to give a fake number for Mom's. No way do I want them to call her. That would put an end to my dreams before they begin.

Then I try to watch another chess video in case Dad challenges me to a match this weekend, but all I can think about is when I'm going to hear about the screen test.

The one adult I confide in about my potential appearance on *Teen Couture* is Ms. Amara. I go to see her after school on Monday but beg her to keep it a secret for now.

"My parents are a little overanxious about needles

and stuff, given . . . *my family history,*" I explain. "I just want a chance to do the thing I really love. And this is it."

"It certainly is an amazing opportunity," Ms. Amara agrees. "I'm uncomfortable with hiding it from your parents, though."

"I'll tell them if I get on the show," I tell her. "There's no point freaking them out if I don't even make it past the screen test, right?"

"Reasonable enough, I suppose," she finally agrees. "We also want to make sure you've got some good techniques up your sleeve if that happens."

She agrees to meet with me after school an extra afternoon a week to help me learn more about draping, tucking, and other things that might come in useful in a competition. If I get selected for the show, that is.

On Tuesday afternoon, I get a call from Adele Bonrever that she's set up an audition for me the following Wednesday after school.

"Do I need to prepare?" I ask, nervous suddenly.

"If you've got any other outfits you've made, bring them. Otherwise, sketches will do," she says.

"Oh, I've got plenty of sketches," I tell her.

"Great!" she tells me. "And don't worry. It's all very relaxed. We'll ask you some questions and look over your sketches. Nothing to lose sleep over."

Easy for her to say.

I can barely think about anything else besides the audition all weekend, or the next week at school.

"What's up with you, Aria?" Dad asks me when I accidentally pour orange juice into his coffee instead of milk on the morning of the audition. "You've been in another world for the last week or so."

"Oh, you know, got a lot going on at school," I say. "Tests coming up and all that."

"Are you sure that's all?" he persists.

"Having tests is nothing new," Mom adds. "You're used to that."

"It's nothing!" I snap. "I just made a mistake with the OJ, okay? Sheesh!"

I see my parents exchange one of those *Teenage girls and their hormones making them crazy* glances, and that just makes me even angrier. I get it, my body is changing, but that doesn't mean everything is about me and my hormones. It just might mean my parents are driving me crazy—which they are.

So I scarf down my breakfast as fast as I can. "See you later," I tell them. "I'll be home late. I've got the Chess Club field trip after school."

"When's our match?" Dad asks. "I'm looking forward to it."

And I'm dreading it.

"Soon," I shout from the hallway, on my way out the door. *If I can't put it off for any longer, that is.* Which means I need to watch even *more* of those painfully boring instructional videos to brush up over the weekend. *Ugh.*

"Are you nervous?" Dakota asks at lunch.

"You've barely eaten a thing," Sophie says. "You need energy for the audition."

I force myself to take a few bites of my sandwich and a drink of milk, but it just makes the butterflies in my stomach dance even more.

"I can't. I'm too nervous."

"Just relax and be yourself," Nina advises. "They'll love you. We already know Adele Bonrever likes your work."

"But how am I supposed to relax knowing there'll be a camera in my face?" I ask. "And is being myself enough? It's not like I'm especially TV-worthy. I'm just a regular kid."

"A regular kid whose mom is a celebrity princess who runs the most successful party-planning business in New York City," Sophie points out. "And whose dad is on the red-carpet shows every other week at some chichi charity ball or another."

"It's too bad you have to lie to your parents," Dakota says. "Because I bet they could have given you good advice for the audition."

Come to think about it, he's right. My parents would have been able to give me great advice about being camera-ready, if I'd told them what I was doing this afternoon. But there's a reason I didn't.

"If I'd been honest with them, they'd have locked me away for my own protection," I point out. "Getting advice would have been out of the question."

"Look, Ms. Amara helped you pick the best sketches to show them," Matt says. "Don't worry. You'll slay."

"Thanks," I say, hoping like anything that he's right.

Adele Bonrever's office is in Hell's Kitchen, or Clinton, as it's known now that it's gentrified and trendy. I'm buzzed into her office, which is on the second floor of a nice old brownstone.

"Hi, I'm Eliot, Ms. Bonrever's assistant," says the

young man who greets me at the door. "You must be . . ." He checks his clipboard. "Aria Thornbrier."

"That's me."

"Great. Adele's just finishing up with the previous audition. Have a seat here," he says, pointing to a chair in the hallway. "I'll be out to get you shortly."

I sit down to wait as he opens a door at the end of the corridor and disappears behind it.

The hallway is lined with pictures of people Adele has cast in shows. I don't have a professional head shot like the framed examples on the wall. All I have is a profile picture I printed from Instagram, my school-made skirt, my sketches, and my sparkling personality, which right now is more scared than sparkle-tastic.

I'm getting dry mouth from nerves. Luckily, they have a water cooler. I take a little snow-cone-shaped paper cup from the dispenser and fill it with cold water. I'm in midswallow when the door at the end of the hall opens and Eliot comes out, calling my name, which startles me into choking. Water comes out of my nose, which is really attractive and particularly embarrassing because the person who was auditioning before me is a guy, and not just that—a really cute guy. Scratch that—drop-dead gorgeous. And I might actually drop dead because he's not doing anything to help me while I stand here choking. Instead, he stands there looking at me curiously, the way an anthropologist might watch an ant carrying a very heavy load back to the colony.

Fortunately, Eliot rushes to pat me on the back, and when I finally manage to breathe again, he offers me a tissue from the box on his desk.

"Sorry," I wheeze. "Water . . . went down the wrong way."

"Are you okay to go in now?" Eliot asks. "Ms. Bonrever is ready for you."

I manage a breath without coughing. "Sure. Ready as I'll ever be."

Picking up my backpack, I head for the doorway of the audition room. Something makes me glance back before I go in, and when I do, the gorgeous guy is staring at me with his light-blue eyes. He grins suddenly, revealing a mouthful of perfect white teeth, and winks at me, like he's my best friend wishing me luck.

His smile gives me a bit of a flutter. But it seems strange after the way he just watched me choke without doing anything to help. Still, there's no disputing his

one-hundred-degree hotness, so I smile back before turning my focus back to the door and the audition ahead.
I want to be on this show—and even more than that, I
need to win first prize.

Ms. Bonrever is sitting in a comfortable chair with a
teapot and mug and a large jug of water next to her. I
wish I could ask for a drink of water, but I'm afraid I'll
choke, literally as well as figuratively, on the audition. I'll
just have to hope my lips don't stick together.

"Good afternoon, Aria," Adele says. "This is Sasha."
She points to another young assistant, who is standing
behind a digital camera on a tripod. "She'll be taking
video as I ask questions. Did you bring some sketches?"

"Uh, yes." I put down my backpack and pull out my
sketchbook. With Ms. Amara's help, I paper-clipped the
pages that I want to show so that the book opens to those
sketches. I hand Ms. Bonrever the book, and she gestures
for me to sit in the chair opposite.

Sasha takes a light reading, and then after she nods to
Ms. Bonrever, Adele says, "Let's get started, shall we? I'm
going to ask you questions, and I want you to answer me
as naturally as you can. Sound good?"

"Sure," I say.

She starts flipping through my sketchbook.

"I love this design," she says, turning the book around so I can see the sketch of a protest T-shirt. "What inspired this?"

"The theme in social studies this year is the Industrial Society and we've been learning about the big waves of immigration that helped it happen," I explain. "But also the nativist protests against immigrants."

I can't help wondering if I sound like a nerd and I'm ruining my chances of getting on the show, but Ms. Bonrever is nodding her head, so I continue. "Anyway, I thought, wow, that's kind of like what's on the news now, isn't it?"

"It is," Ms. Bonrever agrees.

"And the thing is, we were all immigrants once—or at least anyone who wasn't a Native American, which is most people. So that's the inspiration, basically."

As I'm speaking, she's looking through the book, and she asks me about another design as soon as I'm done. Then she asks me some more-personal questions.

"Do you have any brothers and sisters?"

"No, I'm an only child."

"Does that bother you?"

"Not really. I have a dog," I reply.

She laughs, and so does Sasha. That makes me relax a little, so I risk some more humor.

"And I never have to worry about Mozart stealing my clothes."

Sasha laughs out loud. She must have a clothes-swiping sister. Ms. Bonrever's lips are twitching.

"Well, I think we've got enough," she says. "Thank you for your time."

That's it? Does this mean I haven't been selected? But I thought it went well.

"Um . . . what happens next?" I ask, hoping she doesn't say that I'm a total loser who should never darken her doorstep again.

"I've got a few more auditions to wrap up today, and then I'll be making recommendations to the producers of the show tomorrow. They may want another callback, or they might decide to go ahead because of the tight shooting schedule."

She smiles and hands me back my sketchbook.

"We'll be in touch."

I walk out the door trying to decipher her smile and the way she said it. Was it a brush-off or a "you rocked my socks with your awesomeness—we are so DEFINITELY going to be in touch"?

There's a girl sitting in one of the waiting chairs, trying not to look nervous.

"It's not so bad," I tell her.

"Who says I think it's going to be bad?" she says, like I just dissed her.

"Oh. Um. No one . . . Well, break a leg," I say.

"Are you crazy? Why are you telling me to—"

"It means 'good luck' in theaterspeak," Eliot explains hastily, because the girl's now standing up and looking like she's ready to break *my* leg.

It's time to exit stage whatever-direction-is-the-fastest-way-to-the-door and hope that I get chosen.

Chapter Five

"THAT'S NEW YORK IN A NUTSHELL," SOPHIE
says, laughing, when I tell my friends the break-a-leg
story the next day before school. We're chilling on the
sidewalk outside before we have to go in.

"Emphasis on the nut part," Matt jokes.

"I'd have run away screaming," Nina says with a
shiver. "I don't know if I'll ever feel at home here. Everyone seems so . . . angry."

"Like the people at home in the woods aren't angry?"
Dakota argues. "Our step-grandmother convinced
Grandpa to send Dad and Aunt Gretel into the woods

to die, and he agreed, which doesn't exactly make him Father of the Year. So Dad and Aunt Gretel ended up in the house of some wacko cannibal lady who was going to bake Dad into a pie and do the same to Aunt Gretel when she'd finished."

"I guess it doesn't matter where you live," I say. "There's always going to be someone who is angry about something."

"You're probably right," Nina says with a sigh. "It just seems like there are so many *more* angry people here."

"That's because there are more people here, period," Matt says. "It's a city."

"Really?" Sophie says as a taxi driver leans on the horn, almost deafening us, because a car cut him off. "I hadn't noticed!"

Dakota laughs. "So when do you find out if you were selected?"

"I don't know," I say. "Soon, I hope. The suspense is killing me. And you know what makes it even worse?"

"Being afraid that girl's going to break your leg?" Nina asks.

"No, the fact that Dad keeps challenging me to play chess and I don't think I can put him off much longer."

Unanimous laughter isn't the supportive response I was hoping for—but it's what I get. Is it any surprise that I start the school day in a bad mood?

We have to turn our phones off during the school day, but when I turn mine on before Couture Club, there's a voice mail from a number I don't recognize.

"Hi, Aria, this is Adele Bonrever—my clients loved your tape, and I'm delighted to tell you that you've been cast in *Teen Couture*. Taping starts a week from Saturday. Give my assistant Eliot a call, and he'll send you all the paperwork. And congratulations!"

I let out a scream. "OHMIGOSH!" I exclaim, playing the message again on speaker so everyone can hear. "They chose me! I'm going to be on *Teen Couture*!"

"Oh, Aria! How exciting!" Ms. Amara says, her face lighting up brighter than the Rockefeller Center Christmas tree.

Nina gives me a big hug. "Amazing! You're going to be a superstar!"

"Will you remember us little people when you're a famous celebrity?" Matt says.

"I'll think about it," I tease, channeling my inner diva. "It depends on how hard you grovel."

"Feel free to forget me," Dakota says. "I don't do groveling."

"Who are you again?" I ask. "Do I know you?"

Dakota grins. "See, she hasn't even been on TV and it's already happening."

"Don't worry," I tell him. "Sophie will make sure I don't get a big head."

"I'm sure the whole school will be supportive," Ms. Amara says, "*and* help you stay levelheaded."

I realize with horror that she's planning to put my good news in the announcements, which means that that news will get back to my parents—and I promised Ms. Amara that I'd tell them if I was selected.

There's no way I can do that, because they won't let me do it. Besides, then they'll know that I've been lying to them about going to Chess Club. I'll be in double trouble.

I end up messing up the hem on my skirt because I'm so busy worrying about what to do, and have to unpick it and resew it.

"I better not mess up like this on *Teen Couture*," I say to Nina as I attack the stitches on the bad seam. "It would be so embarrassing."

"Embarrassment would be the least of your problems. You should be more worried about being voted off the show."

"That's if I even get to be on the show," I say. "How do I get Ms. Amara not to announce that I've been chosen? If she does, I'm dead. And that's without pricking my finger on anything."

"Can't you talk to her?" Nina asks.

"I already did, before I auditioned. I promised to tell Mom and Dad if I got on the show."

"Oh. That's not good," Nina says.

"Tell me something I don't know," I say with a sigh. "Like how to solve the problem."

"Problem? What problem?" Matt says. "You're going to be famous."

I explain my dilemma. He thinks for a moment and then snaps his fingers in front of my nose.

"Abracadabra! Problem gone!" he says. "Just call me your fairy godbrother."

"How, exactly, is my problem gone?" I ask.

"You tell Ms. Amara that you just got the paperwork and it says you aren't allowed to disclose your participation in said broadcast until given permission by the producers and publicists or something like that," Matt says. "Make it sound all legalese."

"Fairy godbrother, you are a genius!" I tell him, feeling more cheerful already.

"Can I be your agent?" he asks. "I'll only take twenty-five percent."

"Don't push it. You're not that much of a genius," I say. "But I'll buy you a hot chocolate."

"It was worth a try," Matt says. "And I'll definitely take the hot chocolate."

I approach Ms. Amara when it's time to go home and everyone is leaving.

"Um . . . would you mind holding off on the announcement?" I ask.

She looks me straight in the eye, and I'm tempted to look away, but then she'll know I'm working on Lie Number 5 or 6 or whatever it is.

Look honest, I tell myself. I try hard not to blink.

"This wouldn't be about keeping your participation a secret from your parents, would it?" she asks with a skeptically raised eyebrow.

"No, of course not. I've already texted my parents," I lie, willing my eyes to stay wide and innocent. "It's just that the producers sent me an e-mail with all the paperwork, and it says that I'm not supposed to disclose or publicize my participation in the show. Something about publicity and letting the PR company 'build the buzz' or whatever."

"I see," Ms. Amara says, although she sounds only

about 70 percent convinced. But it's enough. "Well, I guess we'll have to keep it a Couture Club secret, then, won't we?"

"For now, at least," I say. "It'll be public soon enough."

Hopefully not too soon, I think. The longer I can keep my parents from finding out, the better.

Saturday morning my luck finally runs out. Dad wants to play chess and I have no legit reason to put him off anymore. I think about feigning a headache, but then Mom will just end up making some vile-tasting herbal decoction that she read about on CharmingLifestyles.com and swears works better than acetaminophen, rather than giving me something "man-made in a sterile factory."

"Mom, we live in New York City. It smells like pee in the subway half the time. I mean, that isn't technically man-made?" I asked her once when I was gagging trying to down the decoction and wishing I had a normal mom who just gave me two acetaminophen tablets and a glass of water.

She looked over at Dad and sighed. "I worry about bringing Aria up in the city, Bernhard," Mom said. "She doesn't have the same connection with nature that we had, Once Upon a Time."

"What do you mean?" I argued, despite my head-ache. "I'm in Central Park every other day practically!"

"See what I mean, Bern?" Mom said. "Maybe we should consider moving to the suburbs."

The horror. The horror.

Luckily, Dad reminded her that there was no way they could effectively run Enchanted Soirées from the burbs and still spend quality time with dearest darling *moi*. #LifeSaved.

But that doesn't help me today. I'm stuck in front of a chess board, being challenged by Dad, who is probably going to realize that I haven't been spending all these hours after school at Chess Club.

I move my pawn e2 to e4. Dad sucks air through his front teeth.

"What?" I ask.

"Are you sure?"

I'm not at all sure. I'm not even the teensiest bit sure. But admitting that might raise suspicion.

"Sure, I'm sure!"

"Okay." Dad shrugs, and he captures my pawn with his next move.

I should have spent more time watching those chess videos.

It takes Dad less than half an hour to beat me. Color him unimpressed.

"What kind of strategies are they teaching you at this school Chess Club?" he complains.

"I don't know." I shrug. "Different kinds."

Dad shakes his head slowly, looking at the board.

"Things come too easily to kids these days," he mutters. "You don't recognize that good strategy can mean the difference between life and death."

You know him as a handsome prince, but behind closed doors, my father is a *serious* drama queen. Or prince, I guess, or whatever.

"Well, I've managed to survive this long," I tell him. "What you call strategy, I call street smarts."

Mom, who has been sitting on the sofa working on a quote for a party, laughs.

"Now you know what I deal with, Bern," she says. "Snarknado twenty-four/seven."

And on that note, I escape to my room as fast as I can, with Mozart trotting along at my heels.

My nerves about the first taping build all week. Between worrying about my parents finding out and being excited and scared about competing on the show, I can barely hold it together by lunch on Friday.

"Maybe I should just call and say I can't do it," I fret. "If my parents find out, I'm going to be grounded for the rest of my life."

"No way!" Sophie says. "Friends don't let friends quit before they've even started."

"Especially when it's something they really want to do," Nina says.

"Not to mention the chance of a lifetime," Matt adds.

"But—"

"Breathe, Aria," Dakota instructs me. "Take a few long, deep breaths. Come on. Breathe in for five counts."

I take a long, deep breath and inhale the smell of lunchroom disinfectant, ravioli (today's special), and my own fear.

"Okay, now exhale it out," Dakota says. "For five."

I breathe out, trying to make it last for five seconds, but it makes me cough.

Matt pats me on the back.

"I don't think I'm cut out for breathing," I tell Dakota.

"You'd be dead if you weren't cut out for breathing," he says.

"I mean that earthy, crunchy deep-breathing stuff," I say. "Maybe I'm just shallow."

"Maybe," he says.

He wasn't supposed to agree with me. Does Dakota really think I'm shallow? Great, another thing to worry about.

"You're going to be fine, Aria," Sophie says. "You've got this. Remember. Eyes on the prize."

"That's right. You want that lunch with Seiyariyashi Tomaki," Matt says. "So you can come back and tell us EVERYTHING, including what he ate."

"I have to win first," I say.

"Exactly," Sophie says. "Keep your eyes on the prize. You're not just doing it for you. You're doing it for us."

I think she's saying that to inspire me by making me feel like I'm part of something bigger than myself, but all it does is make me even more nervous, because now I'm scared of letting all my friends down too.

"I'm going to the soccer game with Sophie and Nina, and then we're going over to Sophie's to watch a movie." Lie Number 10. Or, wait, is it Number 11? I'm starting to lose count of how many I've told at this point.

"Soccer game?" Dad says. "Since when have you been interested in soccer?"

"Dakota, Nina's brother, is really into it." Lie Number 12.

"Wonders never cease," Dad says, going back to reading the news on his iPad. "Next you'll be asking me to take you to a Knicks game."

"Don't get carried away, Dad," I tell him.

"A man can live in hope," he says.

"Bernhard!" Mom frowns at him. "You have season tickets with Dad. If Aria wants to go, she'll tell you."

The thing is, I wouldn't mind going with Dad sometime, because I know how much he'd like it. Besides, basketball is fun and fast-paced, and best of all, it's played indoors in the winter, not outdoors in the fall like football, where half the time you end up sitting there freezing your butt off and being miserable. It's just that I wish he would meet me halfway—like offer to take me to New York Fashion Week or the latest exhibit at the Costume Institute at the Met—because that's what *I* love. Then I'd be all over bonding through sports with him. I'd even be more willing to play chess.

Okay, maybe that's pushing it. But I'd totally go to a Knicks game.

Whatever. I've got to get to the taping. "Okay, I'm off," I tell Mom and Dad. "Argue amongst yourselves."

❁

I take the Fifth Avenue bus downtown and then the crosstown bus over to the West Side to where the studio is located.

After I show my acceptance letter to the security guard, he gives me a badge on a lanyard and sends me up to the second floor.

The receptionist tells me to have a seat, and then a minute later a young man with a clipboard and a bright smile bounces into the reception area.

"Good morning! You must be Aria," he exclaims with so much enthusiasm and energy I suspect he's had more than one humongo coffee with triple shots of espresso. "I'm Justin. Are you ready? I'll take you back to meet the other contestants."

Maybe I should have stopped at Starcups on the way here, I think as I follow Justin down a hallway, trying to answer the questions he's machine-gunning at me. I'm starting to feel way too low energy.

"Here we go!" he says as we get to a door with a sign that says GREENROOM.

He throws open the door and we enter a room that isn't actually green. There isn't even any green furniture in it. The greenest thing in it is the short, spiky hair of a girl sitting on one of the sofas that line the walls, along with a few comfortable-looking chairs. There's also a coffee machine, a small fridge, a fruit plate, and a big basket of assorted pastries that are calling my name despite the fact that I already had breakfast.

The girl sitting in the closest chair turns and looks daggers at me. I realize, to my dismay, that it's the Break My Leg Girl from Adele Bonrever's waiting room.

"Go on, have a seat!" Justin chirps, like Mr. Overcaffeinated Sunshine. "Get to know everyone. Someone will be by soon to take you to makeup."

I take a seat as far away as humanly possible from Break My Leg Girl, on a sofa next to a thin guy with brown hair and glasses wearing a polo shirt with the collar popped and a Vineyard Vines belt. He looks like someone who "summers" instead of going on vacation like everyone else.

"Hi, I'm Aria," I say. "Aria Thornbrier."

"I'm Hugh Waters," he tells me. "The Third."

Are Hugh Waters the First and Second still alive? I wonder. If they are, it must get super confusing when they're all together at Casa Waters.

"Do you live in the city?" I ask.

"Connecticut," he says. He speaks so softly I have to

lean closer to hear him. "I came in on the six forty-three train, which arrived at Grand Central Terminal at seven forty-four. So we had time to have breakfast before coming here."

"That's good. Although those pastries look pretty yum."

"They are!" says a dark-haired girl wearing a necklace that looks like it's made out of the letters from a computer keyboard. "I recommend the chocolate croissant."

"The almond one is good, too," adds Spiky-Green-Haired Girl. "My name's Pez, by the way."

"And I'm Liah," the dark-haired girl tells me.

"That's Mia," Pez says, pointing to Break My Leg Girl. "And the fruit-salad-only chick is Marissa."

Marissa is around my age, but she's light-years ahead of me in the elegance stakes. She's wearing dark skinny jeans with a chunky cashmere sweater and massive pearls, which look like they might be real. And her plate is loaded with fruit salad—not a pastry in sight.

"I *like* fruit," she says, shrugging her blond hair off her narrow shoulders. "Since when is that a crime?"

"It's not. I like fruit too," I say, getting up and helping myself to some. Then I look at the basket of croissants and assorted deliciousness. "And pastries."

I grab a cheese Danish.

But I get to take only one bite before a thin guy with

hair bleached so blond it's almost white pops his head around the door of the not-green room and says, "Aria Thornbrier? You're next for makeup."

I sadly leave my plate of goodies on the table; after telling the others I'll see them later, I follow Blondie Boy down the hallway to makeup.

"I'm Eddie," he tells me. "I'll be touching up your face. Nothing too much—you've got good features."

"Yeah, I guess I'm lucky in the DNA department," I tell him.

There are three people already in makeup chairs, being worked on.

Eddie points to a chair. "Make yourself comfortable," he says.

I'm not sure if comfortable is something I can feel sitting in front of a mirror with lighting that seems to highlight every single skin flaw I have. I guess that's why they want to put on makeup.

The girl sitting next to me is wearing a head scarf, killer pink wedges with a pair of skinny jeans, and a pink blousy top. There's an amazing black patent tote with fuchsia accents sitting on the floor by her feet.

I felt put together when I left the house, but now I feel like a bag lady.

"Hey," she says as the makeup artist working on her finishes applying eye shadow so she can actually look at me in the mirror. "I'm Iris."

I introduce myself. "Do you live in New York?"

"Philadelphia," she says. "My mother and I took the train up last night."

"Wow. So you're going to have to come up every weekend for tapings?"

"Well, yeah, assuming I don't get eliminated, that is," she says. "But I'm not planning to do that."

"None of us is planning on doing that, *jeva*," says a dark-eyed guy with dark, curly hair who is sitting in the chair to her left, having his face brushed with powder. "Who comes here wanting to lose?"

"No one comes here to lose, muchacho. Otherwise the bosses wouldn't have picked you," Eddie says, placing a smock around my neck and starting to apply a thick foundation. "You'll need this so the lights don't make you look washed out," he explains.

The muchacho's name is Manuel Pardo. He apparently moved here from Argentina when he was eight. The guy on the other side of him, a dark-haired, gray-eyed boy who sits observing everyone without saying anything and responds to the questions his makeup lady asks with monosyllabic answers, is called Lazlo.

Then the door opens and Justin bounces in.

"Last but not least—here's our final contestant, Jesse Ffionn."

I glance in the mirror to check out the newcomer and have to stifle a gasp—because he's the drop-dead gorgeous guy from Adele Bonrever's office.

Chapter Six

JESSE WINKS AT ME AS HE WALKS TO THE
empty makeup chair. Does that mean he remembers me
from the tryouts, even though I was nearly asphyxiating
on water? I check to see if he winks at Iris, too.

He doesn't. That means . . . OMG, that means he
winked at me specifically. Me, Aria Thornbrier!

It's a good thing I'm already sitting down, because I
think my knees have gone weak. He's even cuter when
my brain is fully oxygenated.

"I'm just going to give you a little tinted lip gloss,
okay?"

"What?"

"Tinted lip gloss," Eddie says. "To pink up your lips a bit."

All the better for them to be kissable . . .

"Sure. Great. Go for it!"

"I've never heard anyone get that excited about lip gloss before," Eddie says. "Well, anyone over the age of . . . seven, that is."

Iris giggles.

"Guess I'm not going to need much blush, huh?" I mutter, immediately feeling my face flush.

"I'm just teasing. You should hear all of us when we go to Sephora. Right, Coco?"

Coco, who is doing Iris's makeup, nods. "Oh yeah. Eddie shrieks like a banshee when he finds a new color."

Jesse is looking at me in the mirror as Eddie applies fix to my newly glossed lips. It looks like clear nail polish. I never realized there was so much technology involved in having kissable lips. Being a girl is so complicated. The only makeup the guys get is a bit of foundation, a little hair wax, and powder.

"Okay, gorgeous, you're done," Eddie tells me. "Make me proud."

"I'll do my best," I say.

Iris, Manuel, and I walk back to the greenroom together.

I manage to take a bite of cheese Danish and swallow it before Jesse walks in with a guy who introduces himself as Bob Adams, the stage manager.

"Okay, folks, I'm taking you into the workroom, where you'll meet Arthur Dunn, the host of *Teen Couture*," Bob says. His announcement is met with a collective gasp. Arthur Dunn is legendary. He's the director of fashion for Lemieux, one of the most exclusive men's fashion labels, and he also hosts *Chic Cheap Couture*, one of the top-rated fashion shows on cable. Matt was jealous about me being on the show before, but he's going to totally lose it when I tell him about meeting and working with Arthur Dunn. "Then you'll be issued the first challenge. You'll have four hours to complete the challenge, and then you'll go before the judges."

"Do we get to choose our models?" Jesse asks.

The guys all find this very funny. Iris, Pez, Liah, and I look at one another and roll our eyes.

"You'll be *assigned* models by Mr. Dunn," Bob says, keeping it all business. "At the end of judging, one of you will be eliminated from the competition."

We look around the room. We've barely even had a

chance to get to know one another, but one of us is going to be cut by the end of the day.

I just hope it isn't me.

It's not going to be me.

"Okay, everyone ready?" Bob asks. "Follow me."

My stomach feels like it's inhabited by a colony of ballroom-dancing ants as we head downstairs to the workroom. It's a huge, loftlike space with tables, sewing machines, mirrors, bolts of fabric, and mannequins. And on each table, so, so many pins and needles. My parents would have a heart attack if they saw me in this place.

What they don't know won't hurt them. Hopefully it won't hurt me, either. Then I remember that they *are* going to see me in this place, as soon as the first episode airs. If this is going to give my parents so much grief, maybe I should just drop out now. As much as I want to do it, maybe I should just admit I made a bad decision.

But then Arthur Dunn walks into the workroom, and my moment of doubt passes like a sun-shower on a summer's day.

Arthur Dunn is shorter than he looks on TV, but his personality fills the room. He's dressed impeccably, his checked suit tailored to perfection, a colorful pocket square that matches his tie peeking crisply from his left breast pocket.

"Good morning, contestants, and welcome to *Teen Couture*. Each challenge is going to involve making a fashion item out of the materials available to you on set in the short time you have allotted. Now tell me your name and a little bit about yourself."

As we go around the room, I learn that Mia is from Staten Island, her uncle was a firefighter who died on 9/11, and her nonna taught her how to sew. She wants to have her own label.

Liah's mom is from Barbados and her dad's from San Francisco. She first got interested in fashion because her dad loves taking apart computers, which drove her mom crazy because there were always parts all over their apartment. So Liah started taking the parts and making jewelry with them. She's got a decent online business already.

Now I feel like a total slacker. What have I done with my life besides lie to my parents and make a skirt?

As I guessed from his precision with train times, Hugh is really into timepieces. He shows us Hugh Waters I's gold pocket watch, which he carries with him always.

"I respect a young man who carries a pocket watch,"

Arthur Dunn says. "Or even uses a wristwatch instead of his phone to tell time."

Marissa lives on Park Avenue and spends her weekends at her family's farm in Duchess County. Her dream is to have a ball gown she's created put in the Met's Costume Institute.

"I want people to *wear* my clothes, not just look at them in a museum," Pez says. "Maybe that's the difference between Astoria, Queens, and Park Avenue."

Marissa gives her a dirty look. Pez doesn't seem to care. I hope their impending class war doesn't get in the way of things.

"I want people to live, eat, and dance in my clothes," Manuel says. "It's my Argentinean-Jewish heritage. Steak, tango, and tailoring."

"I'm probably here because of my heritage," Iris says. "But that's okay, because I want people to see that you can be observant and fashionable at the same time."

Jesse speaks up next. "Being on this show is my destiny," he says. "Ever since I was born, my grandmother told me this time would come." He glances over at me and smiles. "And now it's here."

It's hard to tell if he's joking or serious. I don't know what to make of him, but he's so adorable it makes it hard to think objectively. There's an unfamiliar flutter in my chest, and I can't help noticing how his hair seems threaded by different shades of gold under the workroom lights.

There's just Lazlo and me left to go, but I'm too busy being distracted by Jesse's smile.

"I was inspired to enter fashion by the pictures of my great-grandparents in court dress back in Hungary," he says. "I want to update that look."

So he's got a Once Upon a Time thing going, too, I realize. But there's no way I'm going to talk about *my* family background. No way. If I win this competition, it's going to be on my own merits.

"I'm Aria. I live here in the city, and I've always wanted to be a fashion designer, but . . . well, let's just say I haven't had much encouragement. I'm hoping that if I win this competition, it'll prove to my family that following my dream is the right thing to do." I look straight into the camera when I say it. It's easier to say to the red eye of the camera than it is face-to-face with Mom and Dad. The camera doesn't cut me off with "But, Aria, you know the tale!"

"Well, now that you've all had a chance to learn a bit about one another," Mr. Dunn says, clapping his hands, "to your worktables."

We spread around the room. I pick a worktable near the edge of the room, because I figure there will be fewer distractions. But then Jesse chooses the table in front of me. So much for that theory.

"Everyone ready?" Arthur Dunn asks.

"I was born ready," Pez calls out.

"Well, then—I shall give you the challenge," he says.

With great ceremony, he takes a pair of gold-rimmed glasses out of his pocket and places them on the end of his nose. Then he takes an envelope out of the inner breast pocket of his jacket and opens it. My heart is thumping with anticipation. I can't wait to hear what our first challenge is.

Mr. Dunn clears his throat. "This challenge is called Home Is Where the Heart Is. Your models are currently entering the room. . . ." He claps his hands and the workroom door opens. The first thing I see is an elderly man in a fleece with ASPCA on it, and I can't help hoping I don't get him as my model, even though I feel bad for thinking that. But then I realize he's holding a leash, walking an adorable shaggy mutt. He's followed by a woman with bright-pink hair and lots of piercings, and she's walking a pit bull.

"These delightful doggies are in the ASPCA shelter

and are up for adoption," Arthur Dunn says. "Your challenge is to create an outfit that captures their personality and will make them irresistible to someone wanting to offer a forever home. You have four hours to complete the challenge, starting from . . . now."

"Ohmigosh, look at them!" Pez exclaims. "I hope I get the pit bull."

She doesn't. Mia does, which I can't help thinking is a match made in heaven. Pez gets a retriever-husky mix called Banjo. I get a little Jack Russell terrier named Flash. Jesse gets a Chihuahua named Cuddlecakes.

"Can we switch?" he asks Pez. "This is a chick dog."

"He's actually a male," the dog's handler says.

"With a name like *Cuddlecakes*? Anyway, I mean it's the kind of dog a girl carries around in a bag while they're wearing matching outfits," Jesse says, making it clear that this is *not* a good thing.

"All the more reason for you to design something for Cuddlecakes, Macho Man," Pez says as she starts taking Banjo's measurements.

Jesse turns to me. "How about it? You want to trade?"

I look into his blue eyes and almost open my mouth to say yes. But then Flash licks my hand and I remember that I need to keep my eyes on the prize. The prize I want to win.

"Nah. Flash and I have already bonded."

He turns back to poor Cuddlecakes, muttering, "This is so lame."

That's *his* problem. My problem is how to win this challenge.

"C'mon, Flash, let's do it," I say to my new furry friend. "I'm going to make you fashion for your forever home."

He wags his tail and looks so cute I wish that I could take him home, but (a) explaining him to my parents would require even *more* lies and (b) Mozart likes being king of our castle and I don't think he'd be down with sharing his crown.

I grab a pad and a pencil and start sketching ideas. At first I'm thinking something to do with hearts because of the name of the challenge, but that's too obvious. If I'm going to win this competition, I can't think the way everyone else would.

That's when I remember that Jack Russells are English dogs, originally bred for foxhunting. I decide to make Flash a country-squire outfit—like if he were Lord or Earl Something-or-Other on one of those shows on *Masterpiece Theatre*. If I have enough time, I'll make him a deerstalker hat, too.

I sketch a design as quickly as I can, then figure out

the pieces for the pattern and how to apply the measurements. Before I make the pattern, I go over to the shelves stacked with bolts of different fabrics, praying that there is something tweedy-looking, but not too thick, because otherwise it's going to be hard to work with on a small dog. I can't find green country tweed, but there's a brown-and-black one that I figure is the closest I'm going to get.

"Plus the brown will match your coloring," I tell Flash.

"You realize he doesn't understand you," Jesse says.

Jesse might be totally cute, but he's clearly not a dog person, which is major points against him.

"That's what you think," I tell him, and as if to prove me right, Flash licks my nose.

There's a big digital clock on the wall at the front of the room counting down the time left. Between the sketches and picking the material, I've already lost twenty minutes. Time to pick up the pace.

Making a bespoke tweed jacket for a small animal isn't as easy as it sounds—especially when you catch a glimpse of the huge digital clock ticking down each second every time you look up. I get the body and the lining sewn together, but then I have to sew the arms. Or is it the legs? The forepaws? Meanwhile, my model has been taken around the block for a pee break, so I can't even try

it on him for size. Trying to press the seams into the tiny armholes with the nose of an iron is interesting. It's definitely easier with human clothes. But I finally manage to get the sleeves sewn and the jacket hemmed. By then, Flash is back, so I have him try it on.

He's not the most cooperative model in the world, squirming like an eel, which makes it hard to get his legs in the arms of the jacket. But I finally wrangle him into it. It's a little loose, and I want a tailored look, so I carefully pin where I have to take it in. But the sides hang down and he's trying to get it off, so I need something to fasten it under his belly. Elastic would be the easiest thing, but that probably wouldn't go over well with the judges. So I decide to make a strap with a button. Flash is getting antsy and I'm getting hungry. My stomach growls every time the cameraman comes in for a close-up and the soundman moves the mic near me. I can see it now—the sound of my hungry tummy is going to be caught and potentially broadcast on TV for all of fashion-forward America to hear.

Do I take the time to grab a sandwich from the craft-services setup off camera? We're not allowed to eat at our worktables, so eating takes away time from finishing. *Decisions, decisions!*

I look over at the craft table. Half the contestants are eating. I could just grab a banana and keep going. Ready, set, go!

My cameraman follows me.

"Can you *not* film me stuffing my face with banana?" I beg him.

He looks at the sound guy. "They told us to film everything."

"You're NOT coming if I go to the bathroom, that's for sure," I say. "There are laws about that."

"Of course not!" he says. And with a shrug, he switches off the camera.

Victory!

I grab a banana, peel it, and start feeding it into my mouth in chunks. My goal is to ingest the banana fuel in under a minute and thirty seconds so I can finish making the strap and start on the deerstalker, which is small and fiddly and is going to take time, but I'm pretty sure will make the outfit and impress the judges.

Forty seconds and I'm only a third of the way through. I have to chew faster. Can I eat without swallowing—or will that make me choke? I try it with a small piece—and manage to partially choke myself, costing myself twenty seconds in coughing.

"You okay?" Lazlo asks, patting me on the back.

"Yeah," I gasp. "Just went down the wrong way."

Liah hands me a full bottle of water. She's already unscrewed the lid for me. "Here, have a sip."

"Thanks," I say, glancing at the clock as I drink. I'm up to two minutes and twenty seconds. Why are they helping me, and how come they're so calm about wasting time on eating?

"Take it easy," Hugh says. He withdraws his gold pocket watch, rather than look at the perfectly huge digital clock on the wall. "We've still got one hour and fourteen minutes."

I almost start choking again. I still have so much to do!

"Thanks for your help," I say, looking around at their concerned and surprisingly friendly faces. Don't they understand that we're supposed to be competing against one another? What about "All's fair in love and war"?

"Guess I better get back to work," I tell them.

Mike, my cameraman, switches the thing back on. I'm starting to hate that red eye watching my every move, and that furry mic hanging about my head listening for every word of self-doubt.

It takes me twenty minutes to make and affix the strap. I should try on the thing to double-check the button is in the right place, but I don't have time. I have to get started on the deerstalker, because getting the ear holes in the right place is going to be fiddly, especially with El Squirmo as my model.

"I hope you're going to cooperate, buddy," I tell Flash. "This is really important to me."

Meanwhile, Jesse is cursing at Cuddlecakes, much to Pez's amusement.

"We're going to have to bleep that out," the sound guy says.

I cut out the pieces for the deerstalker but realize there's no way I can use the machine to sew them together. They're just too small. I'm going to have to hand sew it all.

I find thread, but my needle has disappeared.

"Where's my needle? I need a needle!" I fret, searching all over the table and then crawling around on the floor. I can tell the cameraman is zooming in on my increasingly panicked face, especially when I sit back on my heels and see that I've got only half an hour left to sew this stupid hat that is supposed to be my pièce de résistance.

"There's one right here," Pez says, pointing to the corner of my table.

I stand up, and sure enough, there's a needle lying where I could have sworn I looked less than a minute ago and there was none. Stress must be making me crazy.

"Thanks, Pez," I say, wiping my face with my sleeve.

My hands are shaking and it takes me three tries to thread the needle. *Twenty-six minutes left.* It's got a strange sheen, but I figure it's probably just sweat from my clammy fingers.

I've got to get this hat together. I sew the crown first, trying it on Flash's head to see where to leave holes for his ears. The clock seems to be ticking down more quickly as we get closer to the finish—or maybe it's because my heart is beating faster from adrenaline. Brim. Check. Ten minutes left to do the earflaps and chin elastic, which wasn't my original plan, but I've got to compromise to finish on time.

"You have five more minutes," Arthur Dunn warns us, as if I haven't been checking the clock every thirty seconds.

I'm in a cold sweat as I finish sewing on the earflaps.

I rethread the needle and check the clock.

Two minutes to go.

I can make it.

I'm going to make it.

I can win this.

And I've done this entire challenge without pricking my finger.

I'm putting the final stitch in the elastic and the needle sticks in the fabric. I pull hard, and . . . oh no! I can't.

Not this.

Not now.

I've pricked my finger.

It's just a fairy story, I tell myself. *Nothing is going to happen.*

Blood wells from my fingertip.

I feel dizzy, like I'm going to faint.

I can't faint now. Not with thirty seconds left.

Leaning on the worktable for balance, I find the scissors and cut the thread. The needle falls to the table, but I'm too dizzy to worry about that.

What I do is take the hat and put it on Flash's head, making sure his ears peep out from the ear holes.

He looks adorable, but the floor beneath him is moving in waves.

"And . . . TIME. Step away from your model," Arthur Dunn says.

As I take a step back from Flash, I see spots in front of my eyes, and then everything goes black.

Chapter Seven

THE FIRST THING I SEE WHEN I COME TO IS the red eye of the TV camera.

"Fie the r'd eye," I mumble.

"What was that?" asks Scott, one of the cameramen, who happens to be a volunteer EMT. His fingers are on my wrist, taking my pulse.

"How are you feeling?" Arthur Dunn asks. "You certainly upped the drama for this episode. Well done."

He acts like I did it on purpose.

Scott asks me if I'm still dizzy. I'm not, but when I open my mouth to say no, what comes out is "Nay."

"Quit horsing around. This is serious," Scott says, but with a grin so I know he's joking.

The problem is, I'm not. I don't know why weird things keep coming out of my mouth when I try to speak normally.

"Did you eat anything for lunch?" Arthur Dunn asks. He checks his pocket watch. I feel bad because I'm holding everyone up.

When I say, "I had a little something for lunch," what comes out is "I hadst a dram t' consume f'r dinner."

What is going on here? Did I hit my head when I fell? Is this some strange side effect of a concussion?

"The poor girl is talking gibberish because she hasn't had enough to eat," Arthur Dunn says. "Someone get her a doughnut. One of the extra-sugary ones."

I sit with my head between my legs, trying to figure out what's going on, until someone thrusts a jelly doughnut into my hand. I take a bite, because I'm not sure what else to do, and maybe they're right—maybe I did pass out because all I ate was a banana. I don't remember feeling hungry, though. I remember thinking I had to finish my outfit and then I pricked my finger and blood and then . . .

Dizziness hits again and I close my eyes.

"Take another bite," Arthur urges. "You need some sugar in your system."

I do as he says and hit the jelly jackpot. The sugar tastes so good, I take another bite and another, until I've inhaled the entire doughnut, and then I lick my fingers before remembering that I'm on camera.

It's probably too much to hope for that they'll edit that part out, right?

Arthur looks at the clock and then back at me.

"The judges are waiting. Do you feel sufficiently recovered to present?"

I just nod my head in case I speak any more gibberish.

"Great! Let's get moving," he says, clapping his hands together. "Call the dog handlers to the runway, and I'll bring the contestants down."

Manuel and Liah give me a hand up.

"That was crazy," Liah says. "You just went over like a tree in a forest."

"Yeah, and we were all here to see it, so it definitely happened *and* made a sound," Manuel adds.

"Definitely livened things up," Pez says. "Everyone fer-eeeaked out."

I smile and slip into the bathroom to get a minute by myself before I go meet my canine supermodel backstage.

I can't splash my face with water because that would ruin my makeup, but as I'm washing my hands, I look in the mirror and ask my reflection, "Why am I talking like this?" Except what comes out of my mouth is "Wherefore doth I speaketh liketh this?"

My reflection doesn't have any answers. Now I'm even more nervous about going in front of the judges.

When I get backstage, I check to make sure that Flash hasn't left any traces of poop on his tweed jacket, and readjust his deerstalker to a jaunty angle.

Since Flash is a dog, I figure I can try out the speech thing on him without consequence before I have to speak in front of the judges. I try saying he looks like an English dog.

But here's what comes out of my mouth: "Behold thee, English dog."

Flash wags his tail anyway. For dogs, it's all about tone, I guess. But what are the judges going to think if I sound like I walked out of a Shakespeare play when I answer questions?

"Good dog, Flash," I say, patting his head, except what comes out is "Thou art a valorous hound."

I sound so strange. *Why is this happening?* The judges are going to think I'm a pretentious poser. My time on

Teen Couture is going to end practically before it's begun—and I have no idea why.

Bob Adams gives us numbers—the order in which we'll go down the runway and talk to the judges about our creations. I'm number seven. That's supposed to be lucky. There are seven days in the week, seven colors in the rainbow, seven seas, seven continents, seven spots on a ladybug, and seven notes in a musical scale. There are seven hills in Rome, and there were seven dwarfs in the tale of Snow White, Rosie White Charming's mom.

On the other hand, if you break a mirror, you get seven years of bad luck.

I'm going with the good-luck version, because I need all I can get right now.

Marissa goes first, with a smush-nosed Pekinese, Wen-Yi. She's made her a little pink tutu with pink slippers. The Peke doesn't look amused. The judges aren't wildly impressed, either.

Mallory Anderson, who hosts *Red Carpet Fashion*, observes: "It's overwhelming to have so much tulle on a small, fluffy dog."

"The hair bows overshadow her little face," Josie McGillicuddy, designer of the hottest line of teen accessories, adds. "Accessories shouldn't overwhelm the wearer."

"It looks rushed," Bailey Haberli, the editor of *Teen-Look* says. "The gathering around the waistband is uneven. I know you're under time pressure in this competition, but you can't sacrifice the look."

Marissa starts crying when she comes offstage. I give her arm a squeeze of encouragement but can't help wondering if she's going to be the one who goes home.

Manuel's second. His dog, Brutus, is a cross between a boxer and a bulldog, and Manuel has made an Apollo Creed outfit, with stars-and-stripes shorts and a top hat. The judges seem more amused by that getup.

"I can see that on the red carpet," Mallory Anderson says. "Work it, Brutus!"

Manuel encourages Brutus to walk up and down in front of the judges, and Brutus wags his tail and looks like he's smiling with his tongue hanging out. Brutus is definitely working it.

"Love the top hat," Josie M. gushes. "I can see one of the big pet-store chains picking that up as a July Fourth item."

"It's a fantastic, fun look, but I'm not thrilled with the construction," Bailey Haberli says.

She's tough. I'm getting more nervous by the minute.

Hugh goes next. He has a beautiful greyhound rescue named Dante, which for some reason seems the perfect match for Hugh. He's designed his dog model a Hermes costume, complete with winged booties and a winged cap, and a cape of shimmering gold. The judges love it. When Hugh comes backstage, he's flushed with pride, and it looks like he's grown an inch or two taller from confidence.

"Good boy, Dante," he says, hugging his model. "You slayed out there on the catwalk!"

"Thou shouldst taketh yond hound home," I remark. "Thy puppy dog's so ad'rable and sweet."

Hugh looks at me, confused. Dante wags his tail. I wonder if his previous owner spoke Shakespeare to him.

"Uh . . . what?"

"Alas! Alack! Mine own words art coming out strangely, and I knoweth not wherefore."

"Why are you talking like that?" Hugh finally asks.

I shrug and shake my head, because if I talk, it's just going to be more Shakespeak. He gives me a strange look—I can't blame him—and suddenly walks away like I've got cooties.

Maybe I do. Is this weird Shakespeak thing contagious?

Meanwhile, Lazlo is getting high praise for the practical raincoat with big, colorful buttons he made for his wire-haired terrier, Biggles. The judges can see it being sold in a high-end pet store on Madison Avenue.

Mia's next up with her brindle pit bull, Bruiser. She's made him this biker jacket with a little helmet. I can just picture him riding in a sidecar. Mia may not be the friendliest person in the group, but she's definitely talented. The judges think so, too. There's no way she's going home.

When Iris walks onto the runway with Bobby, a border collie–shepherd mix, I realize with a sick feeling in my stomach that I'm next, and I've got to figure out what to say to the judges when they ask me about my design. I'm going to sound like a total weirdo when everything comes out in Elizabethan English instead of my usual New York–speak. Like I'm trying to be someone and something I'm not.

But I have no idea what to do about it. Instead, I check Flash over one more time, straightening his jacket and making sure the hat is angled just so.

I have this sudden, terrible feeling that the judges are going to hate me and what I created, that everything about it is wrong with a capital *W*. But it's too late to do anything about it. They're already critiquing Iris—things seem to be going well for her.

They're going to hate mine. They're going to hate me. *This is going to be a total disaster. I'm going to be completely humili-*

ated, for everyone—including my parents—to see on national television, and then the judges are going to send me home.

Iris comes back smiling, and Bob gives me the thumbs-up and mouths, "You're on!"

I'm momentarily blinded by the spotlight as I step out from backstage. No one warned me about that. So I'm trying to keep up a confident smile while not tripping over Flash or accidentally falling off the edge of the runway.

After a minute of light blindness, my eyes adjust and I see the judges sitting in their chairs halfway down the runway. Flash and I walk past as we were instructed, and then turn around and walk back to stand in front of the judges.

I live with famous people, so you'd think it would be no biggie for me to stand in front of these celebrity judges. But to me, my parents *aren't* celebrities, they're just Mom and Dad. It's the people I'm about to talk to who are *really* famous.

"Aria, tell us about the thought process behind your design," Bailey Haberli says.

I hesitate. The judges are waiting. There are at least three cameras filming me from different angles.

"Yea, verily this hound doth hail from 'this royal throne of kings'—aye, and queens—'this scepter'd isle . . . This blessed plot, this earth, this realm, this England. . . .'"

I pause, offering an internal thanks to my grandparents for taking me to Shakespeare in the Park, especially to Grandpa Thibault for declaiming his favorite soliloquies on the cab rides home. I'm hoping that slipping in a bit of *Richard II* now will work into the excuse that I hope I can think of before anyone asks me why I'm talking like this.

"Flash doth be an English Jack Russell. Yond inspireth me to maketh a twe'd doublet and de'rstalk'r. Prithee, behold!"

The last thing I want to do is to have to talk more, so I get Flash to do a little circle. He seems to like being on the catwalk and really hams it up for the judges, looking extra cute, like he's smiling. I wish I had all the treats in the world to give him.

"How did you construct the deerstalker?" Josie McGillicuddy asks me.

Oh, this is going to be fun. What I get out sounds like this: "I cutteth out six pieces and did sew the coronet togeth'r first, and then putteth on the flaps, but I hadst to maketh sure to leaveth openings for Flash's ears."

I'm starting to sweat from anxiety. I hope it doesn't show up too much on camera and that the judges don't think I'm a complete jerk for speaking like this, especially because I still don't know why it's happening.

"It's a really great look," Mallory Anderson says. "But I have to ask, since no one else has, what's with the whole . . . speaking-in-Shakespearean-English thing?"

This was what I was afraid of—and luckily, I've just thought of Lie Number . . . 15, I think it is.

"'Taffeta phrases, silken terms precise.'" I quote the one thing I remember from *Love's Labour's Lost* because it mentions fabrics. "Shakespeare is the language of England and 'tis also the soul of fashion."

"Fair enough," Mallory says. Then she starts laughing. "Uh . . . I think Flash needs to get back to the Great Outdoors, stat."

I look down, and Flash is hunched over, pooping on the runway.

"Fie, Flash, ye churlish, onion-eyed hugger-mugger!"

To be honest, I'm not even sure what that *means*. I hope it doesn't have to get bleeped out and I don't get kicked off the show just for saying inappropriate words in front of the judges.

Luckily, when I glance over at said judges, they seem more amused than freaked out. Bailey Haberli is wiping away tears of laughter.

If dogs could look up and shrug, that's totally what Flash would be doing to me right now. He's giving me this *Hey, you dressed me up in this stupid outfit and dragged me out here when I had to poop—what did you think would happen?* expression.

"CUT!" shouts the director. "Cleanup on aisle four!"

One of the volunteers from the shelter comes out with a baggy and scoops up the poop. Flash grins at the judges sheepishly, his pink tongue hanging out of the side of his mouth, like he knew he wasn't supposed to poop inside.

I just stand there awkwardly, taking one last look around the *Teen Couture* runway, because I'm pretty sure this is the last time I'm ever going to see it except on TV. I'm definitely going to be the one kicked off the show after this.

Once the runway has been sprayed with disinfectant and cleaned, someone comes with a clapper and says, "Aria Thornbrier and Flash, Take Two."

"That's a really great look," Mallory Anderson tells me again. "Have you been to the United Kingdom before?"

"Aye, I wenteth with mine own parents," I say. "The fields of England art fair as a thousand fragrant posies. And the warm libations and cakes."

What I don't tell her is that we were staying at the country house of Lord Whittington, the great-great-

great-great-grandson of the famous Dick Whittington, Lord Mayor of London. The place is a cat lover's paradise—they're all descendants of Dick Whittington's cat, Mrs. Puss. That was also the weekend we discovered I am seriously allergic to cats—I ended up in the hospital in an oxygen tent, which was a load of laughs. But before cat dander deprived me of the ability to breathe adequate oxygen, Lord Whittington showed us around the grounds while sporting a spiffy country-squire outfit. Plus fours, tweed jacket, walking stick, the whole shebang.

"Warm libations and cakes?" Mallory says. "Do you mean . . . tea and scones?"

I nod to save myself having to speak anymore.

"I could go for some tea and scones right now," Josie McGillicuddy says. "With a bit of jam and clotted cream."

"You and me both," Bailey Haberli agrees.

Flash barks and wags his tail.

"Sounds like Mr. Flash wants in on teatime." Josie laughs. "Thank you, Aria."

And with that, the director gestures for me to start walking backstage.

Just let me make it back there without me tripping and falling—or Flash deciding he needs a pee, I think.

I do. Or rather, we do.

Iris and Manuel accost me immediately—

"*Ay*, when he pooped in the middle of judging . . . I thought I'd lose it!" Manuel says.

"We were all back here trying to smother our laughter so the mics didn't pick it up," Iris tells me.

I just smile and nod, because I'm trying to keep talking to a minimum. We watch the runway happenings on the backstage monitor. Jesse is in front of the judges with Cuddlecakes, for whom he created the most masculine outfit he could think of—camo gear. The two of them seem to have developed a mutual dislike, which is evident from the way Cuddlecakes stands with his butt facing Jesse and Jesse holds the dog's leash almost at arm's length. The judges like the workmanship but aren't crazy about the design—they think the outfit overwhelms the tiny dog. Jesse isn't happy. You can tell by the way he yanks the leash to get the dog to walk back up the runway with him. Cuddlecakes doesn't appreciate being yanked and runs up behind Jesse and bites the heel of his shoe.

"Twoo wuv," Pez jokes as she gets ready to take her turn on the runway.

Jesse's face is thunderous as he walks backstage. He thrusts Cuddlecakes's leash at the shelter volunteer and growls, "I never want to see that runt of a dog again as long as I live."

"You have to take him down the runway for the judges' decision," Bob tells him. "No getting out of that."

I'm worried about Cuddlecakes. The look Jesse throws at him is murderous. And then he swings around and his eye catches mine, and I shiver because it's as if there's a laser beam of pure, cold anger directed straight into me.

What did I ever do to him?

I rack my brain to think of anything I could have done to cause offense, and I come up with a great big zero—unless finding him dreamily adorable is a crime.

Wrapping my arms around my waist, I take a seat in the corner and review the situation.

First, I passed out. Ever since then, whenever I speak, the words that come out of my mouth are old Elizabethan, Shakespearey stuff. Jesse, who had been friendly to me before, just looked at me like he hates me.

I haven't a clue what's going on, but whatever it is, it's beyond weird.

When all the contestants have been in front of the judges, Bob takes us to another room, where a spread of cookies and fruit is laid out so we can snack our worries away while the judges make their decision.

We're all looking at one another, wondering who's going to be the one who gets cut—but of course no one wants to say that.

Well, except for Pez. "So who do we think is getting voted off the Island of Misfit Clothing Makers?" she says.

"Me," Manuel says. "They hated my workmanship. I'm a disgrace to my *abuela*."

He bites into a cookie gloomily, brushing the crumbs off his jeans.

"No, it's going to be me," Marissa says, twisting a lock of her blond hair between her fingers. "They hated everything about my creation. I'm doomed. DOOMED."

"I don't know—it could be Jesse," Pez says.

Jesse's reply will have to be bleeped if they don't edit it out of the footage.

"We'll know soon enough," Lazlo says. "There's nothing we can do now but wait."

He's right, but waiting isn't easy.

Since I don't want to talk, I decide to check my phone. There's a text from Sophie: **So? How's the next famous fashion designer? TELL ME ALL!!!**

Another one from Matt: **Any good gossip? Famous people? SPILL BABY! SPILL!**

Nina: **Break a leg! And stay away from sharp objects. Well, you know what I mean.** 😊

That's when it comes back to me. . . . The blood on my fingertip. The needle falling to the table, as if in slow motion. The dizziness. Then . . . nothing.

And now, every time I try to say something, it comes out in Shakespeak.

No. It couldn't possibly be . . . I'm a Modern Twenty-First-Century Girl. I believe in science.

It's just a coincidence.

Or is it?

Just then, Bob tells us the judges have made their decision and it's time to head back down the runway. We meet our canine companions backstage and one by one strut down the catwalk for what we hope isn't the last time.

Flash is sitting quietly at my feet as if he senses my nerves. He's such a sweet dog, even if he poops at inopportune moments. I hope he ends up with a family that loves him.

"Well, here they are, your ten contestants," Arthur Dunn tells the camera. "Judges, have you made your decision?"

It's a rhetorical question, because of course we already know they have.

"It was a difficult decision because you all came up with some fabulous designs," Josie McGillicuddy says. "But we did pick a winner."

"The standout, for both design and construction, was Hugh Waters," Bailey Haberli announces. "Hugh and Dante will be featured on the cover of the January issue of *Dog Lovers Digest*."

"Congratulations, Hugh!" Mallory Anderson says.

I want to tell Hugh how happy I am for him. But the camera's red eye is on, and I'm worried how my strange Shakespeare speech will play for it.

So I just keep quiet, grin, and give him a thumbs-up.

Hugh's smile could light up Rockefeller Center. Dante's tail-wagging sends a breeze down the runway.

"But, unfortunately, we're going to have to send someone home," Arthur Dunn says. "Judges, have you decided who is going to be cut?"

"We have," Mallory Anderson says, looking very solemn. "Again, it was a tough choice to make . . . but, Marissa, I'm afraid you will be leaving us tonight."

Marissa gasps but then recovers.

"We'd love to see you push yourself more, Marissa," Josie says. "Try thinking out of your own box."

"You've got talent and a good eye," Bailey tells her.

"Open those eyes to some new experiences. It'll improve your work."

"Thank you," Marissa says. "I'm grateful for the advice."

"Well, there you have it," Arthur Dunn tells the camera. "Join us next week for another round of *Teen Couture*!"

"*CUT!*" the director shouts.

I look at the clock. It's four thirty. I need to get home soon or my parents are going to freak out. They might already be freaking out, for all I know—we have to leave our phones backstage in case they interfere with the sound.

Bob is giving us instructions.

"We need you back here next week—same time. We'll e-mail you anything you need to know about the challenge in advance. Do not be late. Great job, everyone."

As we head off the runway to get our stuff, I decide to risk speaking to Marissa. I'd be a jerk if I didn't say anything, but I'm probably going to sound like one if I do.

"Fare thee well, Marissa. I wilt miss thee."

She looks at me, puzzled.

"The cameras are off. Why are you still speaking like that?"

I wish I knew. But I have to come up with some kind of excuse, fast.

"I allow that it is odd, but practice maketh perfect."

Her impeccably arched eyebrow is still raised. Whatever. I can't stop speaking this way, so I'll try saying something nice.

"May Fortune travel forth with thee."

"Uh . . . yeah. Thanks, Aria. Good luck to you, too." She smiles, and as she walks away, she calls back over her shoulder: "Try not to faint."

Blood on my finger . . . dizzy . . . faint . . . and now all the words that come out of my mouth are from sixteenth-century England.

Something is wrong and I have to figure out what.

I'm going to need all the luck I can get.

Chapter Eight

"HOW WAS THE SOCCER GAME?" DAD ASKS
me when I get home, exhausted and worried about what's
the matter with me.

I stare at him blankly, Mozart sniffing at my ankles,
before I remember that that was Lie Number 10—or was
it Number 11?—about where I was supposed to be today.

"'Twas ill fought. We hath lost."

My father gives me the *What strangeness doth emerge
from your piehole* look that everyone gives me the minute I
open my mouth.

"You 'hath' lost?" he says. "Was this a soccer game
or a joust?"

Ha, ha. Methinks thou doth jest too much, Pater.

As I'm trying to figure out what to say, Dad watches Mozart nosing me jealously. "What's up with him? Were you with another dog or something?" he asks.

Poor Mozart must smell Flash. He's very possessive about his humans.

"Th're wast a stray cat on th'commons," I say.

Dad gives me a strange look but then starts singing something about a stray cat howling at the moon on a hot summer night, and that's my cue to escape to my room to avoid any further questions. While my dad looks impressive in all his princely gear, his singing leaves *a lot* to be desired.

When I get to my room, I immediately start googling speech afflictions to see if there's anything about suddenly being able to speak only in Shakespearean English. But the Internet, usually the font of anything I need to know, yields nothing. Zero. Zip. Every symptom seems to lead to the fact that I've got some awful brain tumor and I'm going to die within the next two months if I don't seek urgent medical attention NOW. RIGHT THIS VERY MINUTE.

The thing is, I don't feel like I'm at death's door. I don't even feel like I'm on the verge of a one-hundred-year nap. I feel totally fine except for the fact that everything coming out of my mouth makes me sound like I'm about to tread the boards of the Globe Theatre in the seventeenth century.

Maybe I imagined the whole thing. Or it was just a temporary affliction.

Mozart follows me into my room, so I decide to use him as my test subject.

"Thou art such a valorous dog."

Ugh! It's for reals and it's not temporary.

I scratch behind Mozart's ears. I wish I knew who I could ask about this. My parents would be the obvious choice, but *obviously* I can't tell them because it would reveal that I'm a lying liar of a daughter who can't be trusted, and I'll be grounded for the rest of my natural life or until I go to college, whichever comes first—

There's a knock on my door. "Aria? Can I come in?"

"Aye. Enter."

Mom comes in and sits on the bed. "How was your day?" she asks.

"One hath seen better."

"Oh? Why is that? And what's with the 'hath'?"

How can I explain any of this to my parents?

There's no way I can do it without being honest. And being honest means telling Mom that I lied, not just about where I was today, but about going to Chess Club instead of Couture Club and so many other things that it's getting hard to keep track. It's a good thing I'm not like Pinocchio. My nose would be so long by now I wouldn't be able to fit in the elevator. I probably wouldn't be able to take the bus even, or the subway. I'd have to walk everywhere. My nose would probably be an entire city block long by now. I'd have to hire people to carry it.

I'm just going to have to come up with another lie.

"I hath encountered Nina in the gardens of central New York, and the lady did convince me to act in the revels by the renown'd bard William Shakespeare. I must forswear normal speech for a se'nnight."

I was able to escape Dad because he started singing that song about the stray cats. But Mom isn't so easily deflected. Her lips compress into a fine line, and her eyes narrow, and I can tell she's not buying it.

"So you're telling me that Dad and I have to listen to you speaking like this for a week?"

Is that what "a se'nnight" means? Oh! Maybe it's Shakespeak for "seven nights." Got it. Ugh, I hope whatever this is doesn't last that long!

"Aye," I say, although I'm hoping in reality the answer is nay.

Mom opens her mouth to say something, then apparently thinks the better of it and sighs instead.

I notice, for the first time, how tired she looks. "How wast thy day?" I ask.

"Busy," she says. "Ever since Snow White Charming ran that front-page feature on Enchanted Soirées, we've been flooded with new inquiries. I knew her site got a lot of traffic, but the response has just blown me away."

"Yond's most wondrous!" I exclaim.

"Well, yes, it is," Mom agrees. "But the downside is that I'm going to be run off my feet for the next few weeks," she adds, stretching out her legs. "And my feet are already tired."

She's wearing these ridiculous fuzzy slippers I bought her for her birthday. They're white lambswool and have adorable little lambkin faces on the toes. I'd challenge you to find a less chic princess item of footwear on the planet Earth. But Mom loves them because they're comfortable. "And they're from you," she always says, but she has to say that because she's my mom.

"I don't want you to feel like I'm neglecting you, honey," Mom says. "So let's make sure we plan some Mom-and-Aria time, okay? Maybe we can go shopping next Saturday?"

Yes! Next Saturday! "Nay! Prithee, not Saturday."

"Why? What's up next Saturday?" Mom asks.

Cue Lie Number . . . what is it now—18? Or 19? I'm going to hire an extra nose carrier.

"I hath a tourney. A battle of chess."

"Oh, that's a shame. Well, we'll figure something out." She gets up and bends down to kiss me on the forehead. "Love you, Aria."

"I loveth thee, Mother."

Mom turns back when she gets to the door. "I'm happy you're trying out for a play. Really, I am. You know I always want to support you in everything you do. But I have to admit, I can see this speaking-in-Shakespeare thing getting really old really fast."

Tell me about it, Mother. You think you're *sick of it?*

I have to figure out how it happened and how I can get back to normal.

But first I have to figure out exactly *how* to figure that out.

Mom and Dad have to go do their prince-and-princess thing at some big Enchanted Soirées charity fund-raiser on Sunday. I could go if I wanted to, but the last thing I feel like doing is hanging around with a lot of people

I don't know and having to make polite conversation in Shakespeak. It would make my head explode. Instead, I accept my grandparents' invitation to meet them for brunch at Foppington's Teacup.

It's crowded, as always, on a Sunday morning, but one benefit of being His Majesty Thibault Rex is that it gets you a table quickly. Like they say, "It's good to be the king."

"I'm so glad you could join us, Aria," Grandma Althea says after we've placed our order.

"Aye, I'm joyous, too," I say.

Mom apparently called Grandma and told her about my latest "annoying teenage pretension," as she called it. From what I overheard, she really called to complain about how it was driving her crazy.

My grandparents ask me the usual questions about school, and I answer, but the whole time, I'm trying to summon up the courage to ask my grandfather something I've been wondering my whole life—and which I'm now starting to think might have something to do with my strange speech situation.

I wait till the food arrives. My French toast is really delicious, fluffy inside and crispy on the outside. When I've had a few bites of sweet goodness to give me courage,

I ask Grandpa the question I practiced: "Wherefore didn't thee just buyeth an extra gold plate f'r Mother's birth feast instead of not inviting the thirteenth wise mistress? 'Twouldn't have cost thee much m're and 'twould have saved a century's w'rth o' travails and tribulations."

Grandma chuckles and gazes at me with pride. "I *told* you she takes after my side of the family. The girl has *brains*, Thibault."

"And you're still implying I don't?" Grandpa says, putting down his fork.

Uh-oh. Over a century later, it's clear this is still a hot-button issue between my grandparents—and I just unwittingly pushed that button.

"I told you to buy an extra gold plate and invite the woman, didn't I?" Grandma says. "But *noooooo.* You had to be florin wise and denari foolish, didn't you?" She turns to me. "King Stubborn. That should have been his name instead of Thibault."

"And you should have been Queen Nags-a-Lot I-Told-You-So," Grandpa grumbles. "Listen, Aria, you have no idea how expensive it is to run a castle. Every year there's something: A leaky roof needs fixing. Stonework needs pointing. Problems with the drawbridge. Repairs to the moat. And that's before the soldiers and the household staff want raises."

"But it was just twenty florins," Grandma says. "And look at all the trouble—"

"Twenty florins here and twenty florins there—it all adds up!" Grandpa complains. "You have to learn financial responsibility, Aria. Don't dip into your capital. It costs a lot of money to maintain a castle."

"That's why we sold the old pile," Grandma says. "An apartment is so much more manageable when you get to our age. Not as drafty, and one doesn't need all the servants."

"Don't speaketh so loud, Graund Dame, thou soundeth liketh a brazen-faced canker-blossom."

Uh-oh. I'm not sure what a brazen-faced canker-blossom is, but (a) I'm pretty sure it doesn't mean "a snob," which is what I meant to say, and (b) my grandmother is NOT AMUSED.

"I *beg your pardon*?" Grandma Althea snaps with the intimidating chill she often reserves for slow waiters and sales assistants. "*A brazen-faced canker-blossom?*"

Grandpa Thibault is unable to stifle a snort, which earns him an icy glare from his queen.

"Pray pardon me, good lady," I mutter. I'd get out of my chair and bow, tugging my forelock, if I could be sure that no one would take a video and post it on the Internet, which I can't, so I won't. "I knowest not what I say. 'Twas erroneous to speak thusly."

Grandma thaws a little. "I can see why this speaking-like-your-character-twenty-four/seven method of preparation is driving poor Rose to distraction," she says with a sniff. "Especially with all she's got on her plate."

Way to make me feel super guilty, Grandma! Now I feel bad about lying to my parents and my grandparents, *and* the fact that because of that lie I've got this crazy speech thing that's driving my mother crazy when she's got so much going on with work.

I debate whether or not to casually ask Grandpa and Grandma if they've ever heard of a speech affliction that makes you speak in Shakespearean English.

Pros: If it has something to do with pricking my finger, then maybe they'll know something about it, because they're old and remember things from Once Upon a Time.

Cons: If it has something to do with pricking my finger, they might get suspicious and wonder why I was around sharp objects, and then my cover will be blown before the first episode of *Teen Couture* even airs, and I'll never know if I could have made it.

Since searching the Internet has let me down, I decide asking them is a risk I have to take.

"Grandsire, in times of old, didst thou hearest of a gent who didst suddenly have affliction of the tongues?"

Grandpa Thibault strokes his beard thoughtfully.

"Hmmm . . . why does that ring a bell, Althea?"

"I don't know, Tibby darling. It's not ringing any bells in my head."

"It sounds to me like a spell of some kind," Grandpa says. "That's what I'm thinking."

Grandma is busy stirring sugar into her tea. "I do wish they'd have lumps of sugar instead of these silly packets. So much more civilized." Putting the spoon down on the saucer of her teacup, she agrees with Grandpa. "I think you're right about the spell. Now I am starting to hear some faint bell tinkling in the old noggin. I can't remember—was it one of the scullery maids or a kitchen maid who was afflicted? One day, every time the head cook asked her a question she would respond in rhyme. Cook boxed the poor girl in the ears many a time before we realized that it was an enchantment that was making her so contrary, not insubordination."

I don't know what having your ears boxed actually means, but it sounds seriously painful. I feel sorry for that poor misunderstood maid.

"So . . . how didst they cure that lady?" I ask.

"I can't remember," Grandpa says. "It was Once Upon a Time."

Seriously? My grandfather goes on forever about Once Upon a Time and how much better everything was then. But now I need to know something of critical importance to my life, and he can't remember the details?

"I seem to recollect we summoned one of the wise-women to reverse the spell," Grandma Althea says. Her brow furrows. "Why the sudden interest, Aria dear?"

Think fast, Aria. Also—lie.

"Methinks should I have to use these words until the day I shuffle off this mortal coil, dear Mother wouldst go mad," I say, which is totally the truth. "But 'tis not a plague that afflicts me. 'Tis a play." That part's totally a lie. Number 20, I think it was.

"That's a relief," Grandpa says. "Because I wouldn't even know where to start looking for a wisewoman in New York City."

Grandma winks at me, takes out her lipstick case, and starts reapplying her lipstick.

"Why, the Internet of course, you old fool," she says.

I expect Grandpa to assert his kingly authority, but he smiles at Grandma with a twinkle in his eye.

"Of course, Althea. How could I rule without you by my side?"

All this old-folks mushiness is the signal for me to make my exit.

I thank my grandparents for brunch, kiss them good-bye, and wish them "Adieu!"

As soon as I get out of the restaurant, I send a text to Sophie: **HELP! Can I come over? It's a 911 but weird and mysterious.**

So this is good. My texts don't come out in Shake-speak. If I can't get cured by next Saturday, I wonder if I can get my personal-device assistant to speak for me.

I ♥ weird and mysterious! Come right over! she replies.

As I walk to Sophie's apartment, I worry about how to tell her about my problem and ask for help. If I tell her I think I'm under a spell, will she think I've totally lost it? Maybe this was a bad idea. Maybe I should have tried Nina and Dakota first.

But Sophie is my BFF, and has been for as long as I can remember. She's the one I've always trusted with my problems.

Mrs. Solano greets me at the door.

"Aria, what a nice surprise! Sophie didn't tell me you were coming."

"'Twasn't planned but a mom'nt ago."

"Well, that's an interesting way of putting that it was last minute," Mrs. Solano says, nodding her head approvingly. "Very Shakespearean."

I just smile and head down the hallway to Sophie's room, because I don't want to have to lie if I don't have to. When I open the bedroom door, Sophie's wearing headphones and doing some pretty wild shimmying to a song only she can hear. Then she starts belting out the chorus to "I Ace My Life," by the Whiz Girls, using her hairbrush as a microphone.

When she leaps onto the bed, I start slow-clapping. She realizes I'm there and almost falls off.

"Jeez, Aria, don't sneak up on me like that!"

"Mine eyes hath feasteth on the dance."

"Say what?"

Sophie has to help me find a cure. I'm sick of having to explain myself every time I open my mouth.

"Thou wert dancing as the wind in a hurricane."

"I was rocking pretty hard, wasn't I?" she says, taking off her headphones and putting the hairbrush on her dresser. "But come on—SPILL! What is this 911 weird, mysterious emergency?"

"Thou hadst better sittest," I tell her.

Sophie plops herself at the head of her bed and looks at me inquiringly.

"So?" she says. "And by the way, why are you talking like you're in a Shakespeare play?"

I start dancing around, hitting an imaginary bell like she's hit the jackpot.

"Okay, you're starting to freak me out now. Do you have some weird illness?"

Since the curse doesn't seem to work when I text, I take out my phone and type furiously, then press send.

I pricked my finger and I think I'm under a spell that makes me speak like I'm in a Shakespeare play. From what I've been able to figure out, the only way to get cured is to find a wisewoman.

Sophie's phone buzzes, and I gesture that she should read it. She does and then stares at me, eyes wide.

"You're pranking me, right?"

"Verily, I wish that 'twere so. Nay, 'tis truth."

"Okay, tell me everything," she says. "Starting from the beginning."

It takes me a while to tell her the whole story, which I do half in texts and half in Shakespeak.

"This is totally crazy," Sophie says.

"Forsooth, I feel like a cockered beef-witted measle."

"A what?!" Sophie starts laughing. "I'm totally going to call Luca that later."

"Nay, prithee do not. We must attend to th' task at hand."

"You're right," Sophie says. "Sorry. We have to focus on finding the cure spell." She bites her lip as she thinks of how to go about that. I hope she has better luck than I did. "Wait! I bet Mom could help."

Mrs. Solano works in the Rare Book Division of the New York Public Library, and she has access to all kinds of strange and wonderful manuscripts from Once Upon a Time all over the world.

"Hey, ho!" I exclaim. "Thou art as wise as thou art beautiful." I think I just quoted *A Midsummer Night's Dream*, but I can't be sure. "But . . . what shall thee bid h'r?"

"'Bid her'? What do you mean by that?"

I take out my phone and text. **What are you going to tell your mom?**

Sophie gives me a *Duh* look. "The truth, of course. How would we make up a lie stranger than that?"

I should have remembered that Sophie talks to her parents about everything because her parents are normal and chill. I, on the other hand, have been forced to be Lying McLiarPants, because if I told my parents about anything I *really* want to do, they'd stop me from doing it.

But look where that got me. My parents may be over-protective, but I guess they have their reasons.

"Who wouldst putteth me und'r a spell . . . and wherefore?"

"People think you're just a regular kid," Sophie says. "And Rosie Charming. But all of a sudden you've ended up talking in Shakespeak. And Rosie went from jeans-and-Converse girl to a walking Très Chic model and back again."

"How now—dost thou bethink Rosie wast bespelled, too?"

"I don't know, but it sure is weird, isn't it?" Sophie says, her brow furrowed in evident concern. "I'm going to have to keep my eye on Dakota and Nina in case some strange Once Upon a Time craziness starts happening to them, too."

"Prithee, canst thou returneth to curing my good self?"

"Yeah, sorry. So I'll ask Mom for help," Sophie says. "But I still think you should tell your parents."

"Nay!" I exclaim. I text furiously: They'll yank me out of Teen Couture before the judges even get to cut me!

Sophie reads the text and looks me straight in the eye.

"You do realize that they're going to find out anyway once the first episode airs?"

She's right, of course. And that's why I have to find the cure to this crazy spell before that happens.

Chapter Nine

"ARIA! HOW COME YOU NEVER TOLD ME you were on *Teen Couture*?" Katie Clark practically shouts down the hall before school the next morning.

Everyone, and I mean *everyone* in the entire hallway, turns to look.

I freeze. *How does she know?*

Whichever friend of mine spilled the beans is not going to be my friend for a whole lot longer.

"Aria's on *Teen Couture*?" I hear Jenna Peasley ask.

"Yeah, I saw her in a promo on Fashion Network," Katie tells her.

I take it all back, friends that I falsely accused in my

head. *I'm such an idiot. Why didn't I realize they would be running promos for* Teen Couture?

Probably because I've been so busy looking up rare-book websites to see if I can find any spell-making books. With zero success, I might add.

"'Twas a secret," I say, having to come up with a lie. "We hadst to keepeth quiet until the promos."

Lie Number 21 or something.

"That's so cool," Katie gushes. "Why are you lisping, though? Did you go to the dentist?"

I nod my head. Lie Number 22 done and dusted, and I didn't even have to think it up myself.

"What are the other contestants like?" Katie's friend Nicole asks.

"Int'resting," I say.

"That's it? Interesting?" Katie complains. "Come on, Aria, give us some insider gossip!"

"Alas, I cannot. Needs must hugger-muggery."

Lie Number 21. My hypothetical Pinocchio nose must be stretching around the block by now.

"Hugger—what?" Katie is looking at me like I'm a total weirdo, but I don't care because I've just realized that if these promos are running, then there's a chance Mom or Dad or my grandparents might see one.

I. AM. DOOMED.

"Fare thee well. I must depart," I mumble to Katie, and take off down the hallway as fast as I can.

I can barely concentrate the entire morning in class, and I don't want to speak because it will reveal the curse. It's bad enough that Katie and Nicole heard me and are probably spreading the word that I'm a weirdo at this very minute.

The no-talking strategy causes major problems when Mr. Falcone, my social studies teacher, asks me what effect the Seven Years' War had on the relationship between Britain and its American colonies. I'm forced to just shrug and pretend I don't know.

A few people start tittering. Mr. Falcone gives me a puzzled look. I'm usually one of his go-to students.

"Did you forget to read the material, Ms. Thornbrier?" he asks, sounding concerned.

There's no way I can explain this without giving the curse away, so I lower my head to avoid his gaze and say, "Aye." Lie Number 23.

"Don't let TV stardom go to your head," Mr. Falcone warns. "You still need an education."

"Burn," Quinn Fairchild says, to the amusement of the entire class. Except for me, that is.

If Mr. Falcone knows about my "star" turn on *Teen Couture*, my parents definitely aren't far behind. I've got to come up with a plan to divert the helicopter parents to a different airport before I see them next. To do that, I'm going to need all the help I can get.

When I meet my friends for lunch, I get Sophie to tell them about the latest crisis in my quest to achieve my designer dreams.

"Sheesh, Aria, your life is turning into a living example of Murphy's Law—everything that can go wrong will go wrong and at the worst possible time," Matt says.

I grab a piece of paper and scribble out the words I want to say. *Tell me something I don't know. Or better yet, help me come up with something to tell Mom and Dad.*

"I stand by my advice—just talk to them," Sophie says.

I'm going to have to talk to them now, I write. *The question is: What do I say?*

"Here's a radical idea—how about the truth?" Sophie says.

I've told so many lies, I'm not even sure I know what the truth is anymore.

"And yet—"

"I think Sophie's right," Dakota interrupts me. "Maybe

they know something about the enchantment."

Sophie explained my Shakespeak problem to the others in order to save me the effort.

"But what if her parents won't let her continue on *Teen Couture*?" Matt says. "The opportunity of a lifetime— gone!"

"What if Aria has to speak like she's in the sixteenth century for the rest of her life?" Nina points out. "And they might pull her off the show if they see the promos anyway. At least this way she's been honest."

I just sit quietly, listening as they discuss the pros and cons, but Nina's pronouncement makes me realize that I should have been listening to Sophie all along.

"Thou art right. I shall bid mine own parents tonight."

Everyone looks relieved except for Matt, who looks worried. He's probably the one who understands the most how much *Teen Couture* means to me, because he would have done anything to be on it himself.

I just hope this decision ends up being as right as it feels at this very moment.

We have leftovers from a fancy luncheon that Enchanted Soirées catered at the Belgian Consulate. *Carbonnades flamandes* with *frites* and *speculoos* biscuits with ice cream for dessert. Although both my parents have asked about my day, they've been distracted by business and a big gala that's coming up in a few weeks.

Some kids have a sibling they resent for taking away their parents' attention. I have Enchanted Soirées.

I wait until just before dessert and then decide it's now or never.

"Mother, Father—prithee lend me your ears. I hast a confession to maketh."

"You've been cast as Mark Antony in *Julius Caesar*?" Dad guesses.

I look at him blankly.

"'Friends, Romans, countrymen, lend me your ears,'" Dad declaims. "Mark Antony's famous speech from *Julius Caesar*."

"Nay. Nay, 'tis not that. 'Tis that . . . I've not been totally honest with thee."

Note to self: Great way to get parents' full attention.

"Really? How is that, Aria?" Mom asks in a low, even voice that tells me she's trying hard not to freak out on me. Yet.

I brought a paper and pen with me so I could write stuff down for clarity.

I've been lying about going to Chess Club.

"That explains a lot," Dad says. "If you played that badly and you were going to Chess Club—"

"Bernhard, focus!" Mom snaps. "So where *have* you been going?"

My hand starts to shake as I write the next part.

Ms. Amara, the new teacher at school this year, started Couture Club. I really wanted to join, but I knew you wouldn't let me, so I lied.

I look up, but my parents are just staring at me in silence. Cold, nerve-racking silence. So I feel compelled to keep writing.

I made this really cool skirt in Couture Club, and one day I was wearing it to Starcups and a talent spotter for a reality show called Teen Couture *approached me to audition for the show. So I did, and I got on. The first taping was last Saturday and that episode airs a week from today.*

My mother's face pales as my father's takes on an angry, reddish tint.

"They allowed you on a television show without parental consent?" Dad fumes. "I'm going to sue them."

"Well . . . nay. I did get Mother to signeth the consent f'rm, at which hour the lady wast on the phoneth with Mrs. White Charming."

"You *what?*" Mom exclaims.

"Rose! How many times do I have to tell you not to sign things without reading them!" Dad shouts.

"Do you know how many forms that school sends home to sign?" Mom yells back. "It's a bureaucratic nightmare!"

Then she turns her anger on me. "And besides—I trusted my daughter not to put one over on her own mother. Obviously a big mistake."

Ouch. I knew this honesty thing wasn't going to be easy, but it's even worse than I expected. It makes me afraid to tell them the rest, but now that I've started down this road, I have to keep going.

"Alas, the tale gets darker and more fill'd with woe," I tell them.

"You're telling us it gets worse than you lying and forging?" Dad says, clapping his hand to his forehead. "Where did we go wrong?"

"What is the worst part?" Mom asks, bracing herself.

Telling them this is physically painful. I can hear the "we told you sos" before I even get the words out. I switch to writing again.

I was almost out of time on the challenge and I couldn't find my needle. And then I found one on my table—

"No!" Mom gasps before I can finish the sentence.

"How many times have we told you?"

"What happened?" Dad asks, his face grim.

I pricked my finger. And then I fainted, I write.

"But you didn't stay asleep . . . ," Mom says, stating the obvious. I mean, *duh*.

"Nay, but th're is a problem."

"Which is?" Dad asks.

"This. I speaketh liketh this."

My parents exchange a glance that I can't interpret.

"You mean this ridiculous speaking-in-Shakespearean-English business *isn't* anything to do with a play at school?" Mom says, her eyes narrowing.

I shake my head to confirm that it isn't.

"You aren't faking it?" Dad asks, double-checking. "You're speaking this way because you can't help it?"

I nod.

"Aye. Verily 'tis so."

"I can't believe this," Mom says, shaking her head slowly. "Since the day you were born, we've done everything we can to protect you from harm, yet you go behind our backs and lie to us?"

Is she for real? Like, hello, Mom, have you ever read a certain tale about a girl whose father got rid of every spindle in the ENTIRE KINGDOM? What about all the women who relied on spinning to earn money so they could help feed and clothe their families? Did Grandpa and Grandma give a minute of thought about all the poor kids who ended up going cold and hungry because they ordered every single spindle destroyed to protect their royal baby daughter?

And as for my mother . . .

I pick up the pen and scribble furiously.

What, you mean like how Grandpa and Grandma did everything since the day you were born to protect you, and you went behind their backs and ended up putting yourself and the entire kingdom to sleep for, what, like a hundred freaking years?

I'm so angry I throw the pen down on the table when I'm finished.

"Aria! How dare you speak that way to your mother!" Dad snaps. "Apologize to her this very minute."

"I didst not speak!" I point out. "I took quill to parchment!"

"That's not the point!" Dad yells.

But Mom, who sits silent and stunned, raises a trembling hand.

"It's not, Bernhard. But Aria already made a good one," she says softly. There's an uncomfortable silence and I hear the kitchen clock ticking again: *ticktock, tick-*

tock. Four seconds that feel like eternity before Mom says, "It appears our little apple hasn't fallen far from the tree."

I feel a teensy glimmer of hope.

"Mother and Father. I'm s'rry I didst lie. Verily, I am. I did want to tryeth doing that which I very much loveth. I have achieved well. . . . The judges seemed to liketh what I hath conceived with mine needle and thread. I hath survived the first round—even though mine own model poopest on the runway."

Dad's eyes bug out of his head.

"Your model . . . POOPED ON THE RUNWAY?!"

I realize he's had a major, and I mean *major*, misunderstanding.

"Zounds! 'Twas not a woman, Father, 'twas a hound!"

Mom, who has been looking like she's about to cry, suddenly bursts out laughing. Not just a little giggle, either. Serious losing-it-till-she-can-barely-breathe laughter.

It sets Dad and me off too. Because even though Flash pooping right in front of the judges didn't seem that funny at the time, it really is when you look back on it.

"I wish I could have seen the judges' faces," Mom gasps.

"Forget the judges," Dad says. "I'd have liked to have seen *Aria's* face."

"Thou hast thy chance next Monday," I tell him.

And then I'm not laughing anymore. I'm 100 percent serious. I pick up the pen.

That's why I need your help. The next episode tapes on Saturday, and how can I possibly compete if I'm still cursed with Shakespeak? And I really want *to win, because if I do, I get to have lunch with Seiyariyashi Tomaki and ask him any question I want about the fashion industry. Do you know what an amazing opportunity that is?*

Dad looks from me to Mom, and amazingly what I see in his eyes isn't anger anymore. It almost looks like . . . pride?

"Brier Rose, she really is your daughter, isn't she?"

"And yours, Bernhard. She fights for what she wants."

"Willst thou help me?" I ask, hope beating like the soft wings of a butterfly in my heart.

"I can't say we're happy about you lying to us," Dad says. "That's not behavior I want to encourage."

"But I think being enchanted has taught Aria a good enough lesson about that," Mom says.

I nod furiously, not trusting my alternative translating ability enough to speak because I want my parents on my side so badly.

"True. And no one messes with our daughter," Dad declares. "I might just have to dust off my nonceremonial sword and polish my armor."

Mom lays her hand on his arm. "Don't go overboard, Bern."

She turns to me. "I'm no wisewoman, Aria. But I will do everything in my power to find one to help reverse this spell."

Mom opens her arms and I fall into her embrace. Dad puts his arms around both of us, and it's one great big Thornbrier-y hug.

I might not end up being the winner of *Teen Couture*. But in a way, I've already won, because I've got Mom and Dad on my side.

Chapter Ten

NOW THAT MY PARENTS KNOW EVERY-
thing, I can revel in my about-to-be TV stardom a
little—but as silently as possible to avoid having to
explain everything in Shakespeak.

"That's so cool about you being on *Teen Couture*,"
Rosie White Charming tells me while we're changing
for Coach W's yoga class on Tuesday. "My mom was
talking about it with your mom last night."

My mother called Mrs. White Charming to see if she
had the 411 on any local wisewomen who might be able
to cure my spell. Even though Mrs. W. C. is seriously well
connected because she owns CharmingLifestyles.com, she

came up blank on the wisewoman front. This is very depressing for yours truly. The thought of having to utter Shakespeak for the rest of my life might well turn me into a mute. My teachers have already commented on the noticeable decrease in my class participation in the last two days. I was tempted to go the Pinocchio route and claim laryngitis, but part of the deal with my parents is that I stop being a lying liar and go back to being honest Aria again.

"I think the guy with the Chihuahua is totally hot," Ginny Krulinsky says. "I want him to win."

Wow. Thanks for nothing.

"I mean, no offense, Aria. I want you to get to the semifinal, but I want to look at that guy right up to the end."

I remember the look he gave me backstage.

"Aye, but . . ."

"But what?" Ginny asks.

"'Tis naught," I mumble.

Ginny walks toward the gym. "Whatever," she says. "I hope he wins. And when are you going to stop speaking like that? It's so annoying."

"Don't mind her," Rosie says. "She's just jealous."

If she only knew . . . , I think.

❀

When I see Sophie at lunch, she's lit up like a firecracker.

"Aria! Mom texted me. She thinks she's got something!"

"Doth she have a cure?"

"I don't know! She won't say. But she wants to meet us and your parents at your apartment as soon as possible after work."

"Tut!" I exclaim. "I shalt expire of suspense!"

I text Mom and Dad and tell them the potentially good news. Mom has a meeting with a new client, but she tells me she's getting her assistant to rearrange it. Dad can't get out of his appearance at the mayor's press conference without causing a political incident, but he makes us promise to fill him in when he gets home.

Sophie comes home with me after school. Mrs. Solano meets us there, but she refuses to answer any of our questions until Mom gets home. I make her a cup of White Willow Bark tea from CharmingLifestyles.com. *A cup a day keeps the aches and pains away!* By the time it's brewed, Mom's arrived.

We sit around the kitchen table in eager anticipation, waiting for Mrs. Solano to reveal her discovery.

"When Aria told us what happened, the first thing I wondered was: How would she have come in contact with an enchanted needle?" she tells us. "I figured if we had some clue about how that needle arrived on the set of *Teen Couture*, it might point us in the direction of the cure."

"'Twas on the table," I say. "My needle wast lost and I did search f'r it on the flo'r. Pez toldeth me 'twas th're."

"We don't know how it got there," Mrs. Solano says. "It could be that there's more than one sharp object on that set that's under enchantment. Aria, you might still be in danger."

"In which case, maybe she should withdraw from the competition," Mom says.

"Mother! Thou didst promise you'd supp'rt me!"

"Not if it means I'll lose you, Aria," Mom says.

"Rose, I know how worried you are, but it might be better if she stays on the show and looks for clues," Mrs. Solano tells her.

"Verily, 'tis truth," I agree.

Mom doesn't look 100 percent convinced, but I'll work on her.

"I didn't have any luck finding the location of any currently practicing wisewoman," Mrs. Solano says. "But I think I can help you despite that." She removes several colored photocopies from her bag. "It was very naughty of me to copy this because of the risk to the original, but desperate times require desperate measures."

We all lean in to look at what seem to be pages from a medieval book, hand-lettered and barely readable—by me at least.

"I found a grimoire in a little-known collection at the library. It was donated at the turn of the last century by an eccentric gentleman as part of his collection, but wasn't considered quite *proper*, if you know what I mean. So we don't include it in any of our online searchable catalogs. The trustees of the library don't want to get rid of it, but they don't really want anyone other than the Rare Book staff to know it's there."

Even though I haven't got a clue what the medieval book says, Mom, who grew up Once Upon a Time, does.

"Renata, who needs a wisewoman when we have you?" she exclaims. "You know how to do research, and that makes you the wisest woman of all. You found the potion to counteract the Spelle of the Elizabethan Tongue."

"Yay!" Sophie says.

"Let us hasten to prepare the potion!" I exclaim. "Go to! Go to!"

I can't wait to be normal again.

"If only it were that easy," Mom mutters, running her finger over the spell as she reads it again. "I'm not even sure some of these ingredients still exist—or if they do, where we can get them. Renata, if you're willing, we'll still need your research skills."

"Of course I'm willing," Mrs. Solano says.

"Snow might have ideas," Mom says. "She has all kinds of sources for her teas and decoctions product line. Some of them are pretty . . . well, *old school*, from what she's told me."

It can be either cute or awkward when parents try to use our terms in everyday conversation. Since Mom's helping me, I decide it's cute, although I do permit myself an eye roll with Sophie. I'm only human.

"We're going to cure you, Aria," Mom says. "When smart women get together, we can do anything."

I look at my mother, Mrs. Solano, and Sophie—their faces all reflect the same determination to find whatever we need to cure me, no matter what it takes. It gives me hope. I just hope Mom is right.

Chapter Eleven

THERE ARE TWELVE INGREDIENTS NEEDED for the curative spell. We have to research the medieval names to figure out what they are in modern terminology—assuming they still exist and haven't become extinct due to destruction of their natural habitat. If they do still exist, we have to figure out where they can be procured.

Later that night, Rosie Charming, her mom, her seven height-challenged uncles, Sophie and her mom, the entire staff of the Rare Book Division of the New York Public Library, a contact of Mom's at the Brooklyn Botanic Garden, and Dakota, Nina, and

Matt are all on Team Research Aria's Cure.

"Okay, we've figured out that Nose Bleed is yarrow, Swine's Snout is dandelion leaves, Witch's Aspirin is willow bark, Lamb's Ears is betony, and Maiden's Cheeses are marshmallow," Mom says, ticking off the ingredients that she's copied from the grimoire. "But we still have seven more to decipher."

Just then her cell phone rings. It's Snow White Charming. Mom puts her on speaker. "I've figured out the Devile's Dipsticke," Mrs. W. C. says. "It's the stinkhorn mushroom. They have them at the Brooklyn Botanic Garden. I know one isn't supposed to take cuttings from specimens, but this counts as an emergency, don't you think?"

"Ohmigod, Mom, are you going to embarrass me again like you did that time you needed that thing for a decoction when I had cramps?" I hear Rosie asking in the background.

"No, Rosie. Because I thought you could help Aria go get it."

There's silence on the other end of the line.

Meanwhile I'm gesturing to Mom to put her phone on mute.

"Thou wantest me to *purloin* rare plants from the botanical garden?" I hiss, appalled that my own mother would be encouraging me to commit such an act of lawlessness.

"Ordinarily, no, but do you want to speak like you're in a Shakespeare play for the rest of your life?"

When she puts it like that, it's amazing how quickly I'm willing to start googling "how to steal plants."

Mrs. White Charming and Mom agree that Rosie and I will work out the details of our future juvenile delinquency at school. Both of these things seem incredibly wrong, but who am I to argue when it's all about getting me better? And to think I was worried about Nina. *I'm* the one who is so easily led astray.

Rosie approaches me the next morning when I'm standing outside school with Dakota, Nina, and Sophie.

"Hey, Aria—I was wondering if we could talk about our . . ." Her voice trails off because she doesn't know if my other friends have been informed about the Great Fungus Heist.

"Th' botany burglary? Th' herbal heist?" I say, like it's no biggie and I'm not at all worried about my upcoming life of crime. "Prithee, continue."

"Say *what?*" Dakota exclaims. That's a pretty New

York phrase for a boy from the backwoods of Canada. It's cute how quickly he's learning.

Nina's mouth is a pink O of dismay. Sophie, on the other hand looks curious and a little excited.

Adventurous is her middle name. Not really. It's Claire. But that's what it should be.

Rosie explains that Mrs. White Charming worked out the Devile's Dipsticke is this rare stinky fungus that can be found at the Brooklyn Botanic Garden and that our mothers, who are supposed to be our role models for living on the straight and narrow, have directed us to go steal one.

"But you can't *steal*," Nina says. "What if you get caught? And put in jail? Can't you just *ask* them for a sample?"

"Yeah, like anyone besides us is going to believe a story about Aria pricking her finger on a needle and being under a Shakespeak spell," Rosie points out.

"I guess," Nina admits. "We're not in Canada anymore."

She sounds homesick. I make a mental note to do something fun for her when the current crisis is over.

Dakota, on the other hand, has already brought up

a map of the Brooklyn Botanic Garden on his phone. "It's a pretty big place. How are we going to find this plant?"

If I'm an apple that hasn't fallen far from my mom's tree, the same is true for Sophie. She's on that in seconds.

"Easy peasy. There's a searchable plant database," she says, showing Dakota on her phone.

"Aria—you're the fashion designer. How do I dress for plant purloining?" Rosie asks. "Camouflage? Top-to-toe black?"

"This knavery shall be done under the light of the sun, so nay t'black," I advise. "Although 'tis Brooklyn, methinks peradventure black doth maketh sense."

"Aria needs this plant. So we have to go after school *today*," Sophie says in her no-nonsense tone. "What you're wearing now is fine."

Thus ends the discussion on the finer points of robbery fashion.

We meet after school and take the subway to Brooklyn.

I was nervous about lying to my parents, but this is a whole different kind of wrong I'm about to commit. And I'm dragging my friends into it with me. But strangely, Dakota and Sophie aren't acting like they're being dragged. They are strategizing together like Bonnie and Clyde.

"I'm worried about Dakota," Nina tells Rosie and me in an undertone. "He seems to be enjoying this life of about-to-be crime a little too much."

"Perchance thou knowest how he hath felt about thee falsing to aideth me," I say.

The shock on Nina's face tells me this hadn't occurred to her.

Rosie laughs. "I think it's more that he's enjoying being with Sophie."

Dakota and Sophie?

But as I look at them plotting, their heads almost touching, sitting on the subway seat just a little closer together than usual, I think Rosie might have a point.

Just before the entrance gates, Dakota and Sophie reveal our strategy.

"Rosie, Nina, and I are going to create a diversion," Sophie explains.

"Oh, do you want me to do my fairest-in-the-land thing?" Rosie asks. "It's kind of a two-edged sword, but when Mom pulled it on the guard at the New York Botanical Garden, it worked like magic."

"You could do that, and maybe Nina could pretend to faint or something?" Sophie suggests.

"I'm so nervous I may not have to pretend," Nina says.

"Meanwhile, Aria and I will go steal the plant," Dakota says, giving me an encouraging smile.

"How dost thou propose to commit such knavery?" I ask. "Rip 'tout the grind? What if 't be true they hast security cameras?"

Dakota grins. "Luckily for you, a Canuck backwoodsman always comes prepared. I borrowed some scissors from Ms. Amara. And if there's a security camera, we've got this. Mr. Seale loaned it to me because I said I needed it for an experiment."

He pulls out a laser pointer that our science teacher sometimes uses to point on the whiteboard. Mr. Seale has to limit how much he uses it, because kids end up making *Star Wars* jokes for half the period.

"When we have our diversion, you and I will enter the conservatory. You shine the laser at the camera to disable it, and I'll nab the plant," Dakota says.

"What if 't be true I don't disable th' thing properly? Alloweth me knoweth and I shall purloin the plant," I suggest.

Dakota and Sophie exchange a glance.

"We figured it was safer to let Dakota handle the scissors," Sophie says. "Given the circumstances."

"Verily, methinks thou hast a point, thou wayward miscreant!"

Everyone laughs.

"Good one," Dakota says.

We fist-bump for luck and make our way to the entrance.

Because we have student IDs, we get in for half price.

"It's a steal," Rosie quips.

"Rosie!" Nina gasps.

"Lighten up, Nina," Sophie says. "She's being punny!"

Nina is right. I don't think she will have to pretend to faint. She looks so pale and anxious, she might pass out before we even get to the right place.

I'm not sure if it's good or bad that the gardens aren't that crowded. There's an elderly couple sitting on a bench holding hands and watching the ducks on the pond.

There's a crowd of people with babies in strollers—it's hard to tell if they're parents or nannies or mannies. They're all chatting away as they power walk around the path and the babies either sleep or watch the world passing by.

"Oh no, there's a security guard," squeaks Nina.

"Just act naturally," Rosie says.

Is it my imagination or do his eyes narrow in suspicion as he walks toward us?

But when Sophie gives him a cheerful "Hi!" and Dakota says "Good afternoon, sir!" he responds with a smile and "Enjoy your visit."

Still, I join Nina with a sigh of relief after he walks past.

When we reach the Warm Temperate Pavilion, I take out my phone. I've got a bunch of pictures of the plant we want so I can identify it.

There's a security guard near the entrance. Nina, Rosie, and Sophie get ready to start the distraction. Dakota and I pull up our hoodies, then go into the pavilion and locate the security camera.

I text **Package is here** to Rosie.

Play is starting GTG, she texts back.

"'Tis fine," I tell Dakota.

I turn on the laser and, covering my face with my other hand, point it toward the eye of the security camera. "Hasten! Away!"

I hear Dakota rustling around behind me, then a *snick*. A minute later he's back with a plastic bag with the strange-looking fungus inside.

"Mission accomplished," he says.

"Parting is such sweet sorrow."

"Okay, drama queen," he says. "Let's make like a banana and split."

I turn off the laser, and as we walk out of the pavilion, we both pull down our hoodies.

"I am *SO* the fairest of them all!"

"No WAY! I am. Sherman, TELL HER!"

I can tell from the voices that it's Rosie and Sophie. Dakota and I glance at each other.

"Who is Sherman?" he asks in a low voice.

I shrug. I have no idea either.

"I . . . Ladies, please, you are both beautiful. . . . I—"

"Come on, guys, you're putting Sherman in an awkward position. Let's GO!"

Rosie and Sophie are in the middle of a screaming contest in front of a clearly bemused security guard and a newly energized Nina, who seems to have grown into her role as the long-suffering friend trying to get her embarrassing besties to stop making a scene in a public place.

Dakota cups his hands together and blows, making an owl hoot noise, which Nina clearly recognizes.

"We *really* have to *GO* now," she tells Sophie and Rosie. "I mean *REALLY*."

"Bye, Shermie," Rosie says, blowing him a kiss over her shoulder as she walks away. "I know you really think *I'm* the fairest."

"He does NOT," Sophie calls back to him. "Right, Sherman? It's me, and you know it!"

Sherman has his head in his hands, shaking it back and forth, probably wondering what he did to deserve being in the middle of such a crazy argument.

As soon as we're out of sight, Nina asks, "Did you get it?"

Dakota pats his backpack. "We did."

Sophie and Rosie go to high-five, but Dakota warns: "No high fives till we exit the gardens—security cameras, remember?"

"Oops, I forgot," Sophie says. "I got so . . . carried away with being the FAIREST OF THEM ALL."

She looks at Rosie and the two of them start laughing. The rest of us join in and we don't stop until we get to the subway.

By the end of the week we have all the ingredients assembled. Rosie and Sophie come over with their moms, and Nina brings her aunt Gretel over on Friday evening to help make the spell. Since none of us are official wisewomen, Mom warns, "This could get ugly."

"Nonsense," Mrs. White Charming says. "It's a recipe. We've all cooked before. How wrong can it go?"

"First of all, you usually have your underlings do the actual cooking," Rosie points out.

"And second of all, you should have seen when my mom tried to make a soufflé," Sophie says.

"What about that old lady trying to make a pie out of my dad?" Nina adds.

"Pray, do not finish the vile task th' mysterious personage didst commence," I mumble.

"O ye of little faith," Mrs. Solano says. "Never doubt the power of smart women determined to make a difference."

"Remember—I saved your father by pushing that old lady in the oven. He didn't save me," Gretel reminds Nina.

"He said that he *told* you to push her in the oven," Nina says.

Mrs. White Charming, Mom, Gretel, and Mrs. Solano look at one another and all burst out laughing.

"That's what happens when history is told by men,"

Mrs. Solano tells us. "*Her*story gets edited out."

I wonder how my parents' tale was edited. All I know is that everything I've desperately wanted to do in my life has been prohibited because of it.

We younger wisewoman wannabes are responsible for reading the ingredients while our elders prepare them and place them in the pot.

I waltz around the kitchen saying, "Double, double, toil and trouble" in a witchy voice, which amuses my friends. That's actual Shakespeare. It's from *Macbeth*. For once this curse has some advantages.

At least until Mom tells me that while she's happy to see that my education hasn't gone to waste, if I don't stop repeating that right away, she's going to ask Mrs. Solano to find a silence charm.

My dramatic flair is *so* underappreciated.

When all the ingredients have been added to the cast-iron pot and simmered, the elder wisewomen chant some ancient words written in the grimoire. Meanwhile, the kitchen smells like a landfill on a hot summer's day.

"Doth I hast to drinketh yond vile brew?" I ask.

"If you want to break the spell," Mom says.

It looks even worse when Mrs. White Charming gives it one final stir, then Mrs. Solano pours it into a cup, and

Mom hands it to me. The stuff is greenish black with strange lumps, as if a giant with a bad head cold blew his nose into my glass.

I've never wanted to ingest anything less—and that includes liver and Brussels sprouts.

"Come on, Aria—you can do this," Sophie says. "Just breathe deep and down the hatch."

"That's right," Nina says. "You'll be fine!"

Easy for them to say. But I want to be cured, so I take a deep breath and drink the foul stuff.

If you've ever imagined what the runoff from the subway platform tastes like after a storm—you know, the same dirty subway platform that's home to rats and cockroaches—the spell cure tastes, like, a zillion times grosser than that. It feels like every disgusting thing in the world is given a moment to dance a jig on my taste buds. I seriously want to hurl. But I have to swallow it down and then worry what it's going to do to me. Something that evil-tasting cannot be a cure. I bet Mrs. Solano got the wrong spell and this is going to turn me into a werewolf. Wait, you have to be bitten by one for that to happen. Maybe this will turn me into a newt.

It doesn't help that everyone's staring at me like I'm a frog about to be dissected in bio lab—Mrs. Solano's even videoing the whole thing for science or posterity or the archives of the New York Public Library Rare Book collection.

I rush to the sink and dry heave a few times.

"Don't throw it up!" Mom warns. "We don't have enough ingredients for another batch."

Like I'd actually be insane enough to drink *another* glass of that awful slime.

After about ten minutes, my stomach's still roiling and making very strange noises, but at least I'm not gagging anymore.

"So . . . what's the verdict?" Mrs. White Charming asks. "Do we have a cure?"

"Come on, Aria. Say something," Mom orders.

I open my mouth but close it again because I'm afraid. What if I drank that horrible concoction for nothing?

"Aria, honey, please," Mom says, gentler this time. "We need to know if this worked."

I need to know too.

So I open my mouth and say exactly that I'm thinking: "That made Mrs. White Charming's wood-betony-and-kelp smoothie taste like a chocolate Frappuccino with extra caramel sauce." I smile at Mrs. White Charming. "No offense."

"No offense taken," Mrs. W. C. says, smiling and high-fiving Mrs. Solano.

Mom hugs me so hard she almost squeezes the words out of me. "I'm so glad we could cure you, Aria!" she says. "I was scared that you'd be under that awful curse forever."

"You think *you're* glad," I say. "That Shakespeak was getting really old."

"More like old-fashioned," Sophie quips.

"I still don't understand why anyone would hate me enough to put a curse on me," I say.

"Hate doesn't need a logical reason," Mom says. "It festers and grows until it becomes completely illogical."

"Love is a much better thing to spread," Mrs. White Charming says.

That all sounds great in theory.

But I still face two big problems: Namely, I need to figure out who did this to me, and more important, how to win *Teen Couture*.

Chapter Twelve

EVEN THOUGH I'M CURED, IT'S STILL A
battle to get my parents to let me continue to compete
on *Teen Couture*—especially since we still don't know
who planted the needle on set. Dad wants to accom-
pany me to Saturday's taping dressed in chain mail
and sporting his newly sharpened battle sword, but
Mom and I manage to convince him that this (a) isn't
the most subtle approach, (b) might get him arrested,
and (c) might possibly get him locked up in a psych
ward.

I beg Mom and Dad to let me go by myself, but that's
a nonstarter.

"Don't you understand, Aria?" Mom said. "You could have been *killed!*"

She has a *point. Hahahaha.* Get it?

I think that's what's known as gallows humor.

And that's how I end up in a taxi on the way to the studio with my grandparents, who are the compromise chaperones. I barely slept last night, worrying about all the un-PC things they might say on camera, which are bound to get me kicked off the show. I try to give them some helpful hints on the ride over:

"Remember, Grandma and Grandpa, this show is called *Teen Couture*, not *Lifestyles of the Rich and Royal*, okay?" I warn them. "So please don't make loud comments about how uncouth and common things are or anything like that. I don't want the other contestants coming after me with scissors and glue guns because you've made some let-them-wear-polyester comment."

Grandma Althea turns to Grandpa Thibault. "From what I understand, Tibby, we are to sit without moving or speaking."

"Like the guards at Buckingham Palace," Grandpa Thibault says. "Always seemed a bit over the top to me, but tradition is tradition."

"You can speak," I say. "As long as you don't say the wrong things."

"Perhaps you should give us a list of what we can and can't say," Grandma says. "I get confused about what's in and what's out these days."

Sometimes I feel like my grandparents aren't just from Once Upon a Time—they're from another planet. I mean, my grandmother is convinced to this day that she found out she was going to have Mom from a talking frog while she was taking a swim in a river near the palace. Pretty out there, am I right?

"Can I ask you a question?" I say.

"This is a democracy, not a monarchy, more's the pity," Grandpa Thibault says. "Fire away."

"It's something I've been thinking about a lot— especially since all this happened to me," I say.

"Go on," Grandma says. "I'm all agog."

"You destroyed all the spindles in the kingdom to protect Mom from the curse that Floriana Foxglove cast on her at that party," I remind them. "Even though that destroyed the livelihoods of thousands of women in the kingdom."

"Well . . . yes," Grandpa Thibault harrumphs. "What would you have done, Aria? She was our only child. We'd been trying for a child for years."

"Yeah, I know, and then Grandma found out from the talking frog that she would have a daughter before the year was out. I've heard the tale more than once."

"So then you can understand how we couldn't bear to lose her," Grandma says.

I don't know what I would have done—it's not that I blame my grandparents for wanting to save their daughter, and I'm obviously glad Mom's alive because otherwise I wouldn't be here. But I still wonder what happened to all the women who relied on their spindles to make a living.

"Okay, but what about her fifteenth birthday? Floriana Foxglove specifically said that Mom would prick her finger when she turned fifteen, but instead of keeping an eye on her that day, you guys go off and *leave her alone* at the palace," I remind them. "I mean seriously, Gramps— *what were you thinking?*"

Grandma gives a bitter laugh.

"That's exactly what *I* said when Thibault told me we were going to open the new crossbow factory on the southern border," Grandma says. "I asked him if he'd forgotten that not only was it Rose's birthday, it was her *fifteenth* birthday. I told him we should be with her, to keep her out of trouble. But no . . . he was convinced that not one spindle remained in the land, because he's the king and who would dare to disobey him?"

"Um . . . Mom?" I point out.

"Your grandmother likes to blame me for every-thing," Grandpa says. He sounds particularly grumpy. "But that's what I didn't count on. I trusted Rose. She was a good kid. She followed the rules. She knew about the curse. Why would she disobey me when she knew it would put her at risk?"

"Indeed, why would she?" Grandma asks, looking at me pointedly.

Ouch.

"I don't know . . . maybe because she was curious?" I finally find the courage to say. "Because it was something she'd never been allowed to do but she thought it was something she'd really love doing? Maybe she wanted to be creative instead of just being Princess Rose and hav-ing all these gold-digging, power-hungry princes show-ing up, wanting to marry her just so they could inherit the kingdom?"

When I finish, I wonder whether this is going to cause an earthquake. I've never spoken to my grandparents this bluntly before.

The taxi driver catches my eye in the rearview mir-ror and gives me an encouraging wink. It's nice to know *someone* is on my side in speaking the truth to my aging royal relatives.

But to my amazement, my grandparents don't get angry and shout. They start *laughing*.

"I told Rose she'd end up with a daughter just like herself!" Grandma gasps in between some seriously unqueenly guffaws.

All Grandpa seems capable of doing is repeating "apple . . . tree . . . apple . . . tree" over and over again.

I'm not sure if I should be amused, annoyed, or relieved. I decide I'm a mixture of all three.

Grandma takes a crisp white linen handkerchief with lace edges out of her handbag and daintily dabs the laugh tears from her eyes, careful not to smudge her makeup. Grandpa removes a similarly crisp blue one from his pocket and blows his nose. I mean, who even uses those anymore? One good nose blow and then you have to carry around a thing full of snot for some poor underling to wash and iron. That's assuming you can afford the underling.

"Aria, I know you think we were 'helicopter parents,'" Grandpa says.

"A grotesque term, if you ask me," Grandma sniffs.

"I'll admit, I didn't handle the spindle thing well.

Trying to protect my daughter caused grave hardship for my poorest subjects."

At least he admits it. I never thought he would.

"But the day before Rose turned fifteen, I had an epiphany. I realized that Grandma and I couldn't keep her sheltered forever. At some point we had to trust her to look after herself."

"I thought it was more sensible to wait till the day *after* she turned fifteen, since Floriana Foxglove said Rose would prick her finger and die *on her fifteenth birthday,*" Grandma says, with a pointed look at Grandpa, who rolls his eyes. It's clearly not the first time they've had this argument. "Yes, Pinny Primrose mitigated the spell so she didn't die. But still. *Someone* had to pull the I'm-the-king-and-we're-doing-it-my-way card."

I look up at the rearview mirror and the taxi driver's eyes are twinkling. He's probably wishing for a bowl of popcorn and a soda, because listening to my family's reality show in the backseat is such great entertainment.

"Was it worth sleeping for one hundred years?" I ask my grandparents.

Grandpa gives me a shrewd look. "Was it worth—"

Grandma coughs loudly and looks meaningfully at the cabdriver.

"Was it worth going through *what you just went through*?" Grandpa continues more discreetly.

He's got me there—if I had to do it all over again, would I still do everything I could to get on *Teen Couture* to follow my dream?

"Yes," I tell my grandparents. "Because I've always wanted to be a fashion designer and I have to try it even if I fail. Or . . . have other weird things happen."

Grandpa's patrician face breaks into a broad smile. "See, Althea? Our girl is a fighter. She might not wear a hauberk and carry a sword, but the blood of warriors runs in her veins."

"Cool," I say. "As long as that blood helps me get through today's challenge."

Grandma Althea acts like a total fangirl when I introduce her to Arthur Dunn. She asks him to sign her reading-glasses case with her lipstick. Luckily, he finds a Sharpie instead.

I never pegged her for a *Chic Cheap Couture* fan. Grandpa, meanwhile, is glowering and muttering about his hauberk and sword. I learn more about my family's weirdness every day.

"You better get to makeup," Arthur Dunn tells me,

waving me off in that direction. "I promise to look after this delightful young lady for you."

Grandma actually *giggles*, which just makes Grandpa glower even more. The challenge is going to be a cinch after this.

Or not.

When I walk into makeup, it's hard not to be suspicious of all the faces that turn to greet me.

One of my fellow cast members put that enchanted needle on my table. It had to be one of them, because it happened in the middle of taping. I need to figure out who it is before he or she tries it again and I end up with a worse curse than Shakespeak. Or dead, even.

"Hey, Aria! How are you feeling?" Pez asks, when I take a seat in the makeup chair next to her.

She seems friendly and genuine enough. But Pez is the one who told me the needle was on the table. Maybe she's just asking to see if I'm still under a spell.

"Fine," I answer, keeping it to a minimum.

"We don't want her passing out again," Jesse says without turning around.

He was right there too. I find him confusing, and I don't think it's just because he's a guy whose looks make my heart beat faster. One minute he's flashing that oh-so-adorbs smile my way and the next he's giving me an *if looks could kill you'd be deader than a doornail* glare. Maybe he's just moody? Or could it be that there's something more sinister?

"Is everyone else as nervous as I am?" Iris asks, taking my attention away from Jesse. "I couldn't even eat breakfast."

Iris was on the other side of the room, so she couldn't have put the needle there. But wait—maybe she gave it to Pez or Jesse and suggested putting it on my table!

The truth is, anyone could have put the enchanted needle there while I was scrabbling around on the floor looking for the one I lost.

"I wonder what today's challenge is going to be," Manuel says.

"It better not involve dogs," Jesse grumbles.

I can't suppress a giggle.

His light-blue eyes meet mine in the mirror. Today they are neither flirty nor killer—they're unreadable, expressionless.

"It won't," Hugh reassures Jesse. "It's always something totally different."

"Yeah, like what's the opposite of shelter puppies?" Lazlo asks.

"Dressing hedge-fund managers?" Mia suggests.

Eddie and Coco look at each other.

"Can you imagine that episode?" Eddie asks Coco. "Having the contestants dress the billionaire guys in bespoke suits?"

"Arthur would *love* it," Coco giggles. "We have to tell him."

"Give me credit," Mia demands. "It was my idea."

"Relax. No one is stealing your idea," Eddie tells her.

"Don't tell me to relax," Mia says. "People steal ideas all the time."

I wonder if Mia is the culprit. She's so prickly all the time—like she's got a permanent chip on her shoulder. But how would she learn the enchantment spell? And I haven't told anyone who my parents are, so why me?

I look around the room at the rest of the contestants: Hugh, who seems so gentle and well mannered; Liah, who seems so nice and caring; Lazlo, who's so interesting and cool; and Manuel, who I can't imagine doing something like this because it would shame his *abuela*. But it has to be one of them. And the fact that I don't know which one makes me feel even more nervous than I was last week about the upcoming challenge. Then Bob Adams comes in to lead us up to the workroom for round two.

I'm going to have to keep my eyes peeled for clues and my hands fisted to protect my fingertips. Well, except for when I'm working, of course. It'll be hard to win, otherwise.

"Welcome to episode two of *Teen Couture*," Arthur Dunn announces once the cameras start rolling. "Today's challenge is all about teamwork. You'll be divided into groups of three for the challenge, and how well you work together will determine if you stay or go."

I look around at my competitors. Great. Just when I have to be suspicious of every single person in the competition for my own safety, I have to work with them in order to get through to the next round.

"The Red Group will consist of Liah, Hugh, and Iris," Mr. Dunn announces. I hold my breath. "Manuel, Pez, and Lazlo—you're the Green Group."

I exhale, my stomach turning over in dismay.

"That leaves Jesse, Mia, and Aria in the Blue Group. Okay, everyone, get together with your group and prepare to hear the challenge."

Arthur Dunn and the producers of *Teen Couture* must hate me. Staying in the competition depends on teamwork, and they've put me with a guy who flirts with me one minute and acts like he wants to kill me the next, and a girl who's made it clear she can't stand me, for reasons I don't even know. I'm doomed.

Jesse and I exchange uneasy smiles as we meet at our assigned worktable. Mia doesn't bother.

"Just my luck to get stuck with you," she grumbles.

I can't tell if she means me or Jesse or both of us, but it gets us off to a great start, obviously.

"I wouldn't have picked you, either," Jesse says.

"Guys, you realize that staying in the competition depends on how well we work together as a team, right?" I remind them, speaking clearly for the mic that's on a boom above our heads.

That earns me dirty looks from both my teammates as Arthur Dunn claps his hands to get our attention. *Great.*

"Teams, your challenge is to dress a fairy-tale character," he says. "You have four hours to complete the challenge, starting . . . now."

Talk about irony.

"So who are we going to design for?" Mia asks. "I vote for the Beast."

Jesse gives me a sly look. "I'm thinking Sleeping Beauty."

Wait. Does that mean he knows she's my mom? He's

just jumped to number one on my suspect list.

Mia snorts. "Oh *that'll* be fun. All she did was sleep for a hundred years. What are we going to do, design her a freaking nightgown?"

"I agree," I say. "The Beast offers more interesting fashion possibilities."

Glancing over at Jesse to see how he's taking being overruled, I see that he's smiling, but catch a slight narrowing of his eyes. Is he hiding something?

I feel bad that Mom's going to see me agree that she's boring, because it's not true at all. She grew up to be interesting and successful after she woke up from her century-long nap. In my humble opinion, her story is an example of why naps should be taken at every possible opportunity.

"Guess you're outvoted, Prince Not-So-Charming," Mia tells Jesse.

"So what's our concept?" I ask, trying to focus us back on the challenge.

"Everyone always dresses the Beast all Olde Worlde and what's the word . . . baroque," Mia says. "We should change it up. Make him goth or steampunk or something."

"I say stay classic," Jesse says. "If it ain't ba-roke, don't fix it."

I groan. "Even if it weren't for the corny joke, I'd agree with Mia. We'll only win if we think out of the box."

"Okay, steampunk," Jesse says. "At least then it doesn't have to be all black and boring."

He looks pointedly at Mia, who is dressed top to toe in black. She ignores him.

Between us—well, mainly between Mia and me, while Jesse stands there with his arms crossed like a pillar of hostile salt, complaining and making snarky comments—we sketch out a smoking jacket with a velvet collar, slim black pants, and a silk scarf with a gear theme.

We race to the fabric area to find what we need. Mia puts Jesse in charge of finding black fabric for the pants to get him back for saying black is boring. She's scoping out stuff for the scarf, while I look for the jacket material.

When we meet back at the worktable, I've got this awesome gold brocade, black rayon for the lining, and black velvet for the collar. Mia's got a bunch of cool fabrics to work with for the scarf, including some glittery, brassy, and silver material to make gear shapes with. Jesse finally shows up with the black crepe for the pants.

We're working with a mannequin instead of a live model this time. Since our character is the Beast, ours is a very cut male mannequin.

I start taking measurements and Mia writes them down so we can all use them.

"I've got a six-pack just like that," Jesse brags.

Was he always this annoying and I didn't notice it because I was too busy being distracted by his eyes and cheekbones and all that? They are very, *very* distracting, it's true.

"Any danger of you doing some actual teamwork?" Mia asks him. "Or are you just going to pretend you're the mannequin and leave it all to us?"

"The mannequin has a better personality than you do," Jesse retorts, but at least he rolls out the pants fabric and starts marking out the measurements to cut.

Mia winks at me. Maybe under the tough exterior that terrified me so much, she could be an ally. Or maybe she's just trying to lull me into a false sense of security? One thing is for certain, though—she's a really hard worker. The two of us are measuring and cutting side by side, offering advice and suggestions. Jesse is working on his own, basically ignoring the two of us, as if we weren't in a team competition. I hope it doesn't count against us.

I'm starving, but when they bring pizza for lunch, I decide to wait until I can eat by myself—so I can be assured that no one will give me a slice of poisoned pizza or contaminated Coke. My stomach is growling so loudly the sound guy picks it up on audio and tells me they'll have to edit it out.

"Aren't you going to eat?" Mia asks when she comes back from her own quick break. "You don't want to faint again."

"I know," I tell her. "I'll go soon."

Mia looks over her shoulder at the pizza table, where Jesse is talking to Lazlo while he eats.

"Listen, watch your back," she says. "Last week after the show, I overheard Jesse talking on the phone in the hallway outside the greenroom. He didn't know I was there, and he was talking about you—and saying some weird stuff."

I go still. "Like what?"

"Like that you fainted, and he thought it worked, but then you woke up." The shock must show on my face, because she continues, "I know, right? That's so messed up, because of course you woke up. Duh! So *what* was supposed to work?"

A curse, that's what. Maybe one that was supposed to *kill* me. Mom's spindle curse was supposed to kill her—it was only through some magical intervention of the other wisewomen that death was downgraded to a superlong nap.

"Good question," I say, although I know what ended up happening instead. I woke up spouting Shakespeak. But what was the curse that Jesse and his phone accomplice intended?

"Then he says something about how maybe it went wrong or something, and it sounded like he was getting chewed out by the person on the other end, because he keeps saying, 'It's not my fault,'" Mia says. "And get this—it turns out he's talking to his *grandma*."

"Wow. Unbelievable."

Out of the corner of my eye, I see Jesse heading back to us. I need to text Mom and my friends so they know this additional information. Maybe they can find something out while I'm here risking my life for a future in fashion.

"Listen, Mia, can you do me a favor and keep a close eye on Jesse?"

"As close as I can while I'm working," she says.

"Just make sure he doesn't do anything like switch sewing needles with me. It's really important."

She gives me a curious look, like she's trying to

figure out what's behind this, as Jesse returns.

I bolt for the pizza, hoping there's still some mushroom left.

Luckily, there's still one slice. But wait . . . Jesse was just here. What if he surreptitiously switched normal mushrooms with poisoned mushrooms? Just to be safe, I switch to cheese instead. After taking a few bites, I take out my phone, turn it on, and text the Double-Double-Toil-and-Trouble group to update them on what Mia told me. Fortunately, the cameraman stays with Mia and Jesse, so I can get away with it.

Mom texts me back right away.

It's not safe there! Get Grandma and Grandpa to bring you home!

Before, I might have been mad to read that, but now I understand. The danger is real, and my mother loves me, so she's worried about me. I'm worried about me, too. But despite the risks, I'm not going home. Not yet.

No, Mom! I'm being careful, I promise!!!!!!!!! I have to see this through!!!

I've just taken another bite of pizza when there's a text from Sophie.

So Mom just found this out. Do you know what Ffionn means in Welsh?

Ffionn? Oh, wait, that's Jesse's last name.

No, what?

FOXGLOVE.

The shock makes me choke on my pizza, coughing so much that I drop my phone. This can't be a coincidence. Jesse has the same last name as Floriana Foxglove, the wisewoman who tried to kill my mother. Mia heard him talking on the phone to someone after last week's taping, saying that he "thought it worked" but then I "woke up."

The clues are adding up, and they all point to the guy who I thought was crushworthy. I clearly have *really* bad taste in crushes.

"Here's your phone. You should probably turn it off before Arthur finds out."

Hugh is standing there, holding out my phone, which is buzzing furiously in his hands.

I take it, but I'm afraid to look at what all the texts say. Mom's head has probably exploded. She's probably on her way here now, with an NYPD SWAT team. She's probably texting Grandma and Grandpa to tell them to drag me off the set, except they still have flip phones and most of the time they have them turned off, so a whole lot of good *that's* going to do.

"Yeah," I say, turning it off. "You're right. It was an emergency."

"Are you feeling okay? You're not going to faint again, are you?"

"No . . . I'm fine. It's not that," I assure him, although my brain is spinning a little with the knowledge that Jesse could be related to Floriana Foxglove, who tried to kill my mother. That the guy I had a crush on might have tried to kill *me*.

"Listen, Aria, I've been waiting to speak to you without a camera around," Hugh says in an undertone.

"What about?"

"Last week after we finished filming, I hung around to talk to one of the cameramen because I wanted to ask him if I could interview him for the school paper. He was reviewing the footage from before and after you fainted, and he saw something strange."

"What was that?"

"Jesse took your original needle when you went to have lunch and hid it in his bag. Why would he do that? I think he might be trying to sabotage you in some way."

"Oh, he is," I tell him. "I'll tell you the whole story. It's . . . unbelievable." I glance at the clock ticking down. "But I have to get through the challenge first."

"Watch out for him," Hugh warns.

"Don't worry," I tell him. "I will."

As I head back to my group, I realize that between my family history, what Mia and Hugh heard and saw, and the fact that Jesse's name is Foxglove, I probably have enough proof to go to the producers of *Teen Couture* and tell them that Jesse is a cheat who might have tried to kill me but made me speak Shakespearean English instead.

There are two problems with this plan: (1) It sounds crazy, even to me, and (2) we've got to finish the challenge first if I want to get through to the next round. #teamwork.

Mia finishes the scarf first, despite having to sew all the gear features on by hand.

"It looks amazing," I tell her.

Even Jesse gives it a nod of approval and grunts, "Cool."

I'm sewing the lining into the jacket pieces.

"Do you want me to start on the velvet collar?" Mia asks.

"That would be awesome," I say, glancing at the clock. "Unless you need help more, Jesse?"

"Nah, I'm good," he says. "Just got to get the waistband and zipper in and then hem the legs."

We're a team of sorts, I guess, despite the fact that one of my teammates might well have tried to kill me. I just hope we're working together well enough to keep us in the competition.

By the time Arthur Dunn announces we're fifteen minutes away from the end of the challenge, we've got a pretty decent Beast outfit, but the fact that Jesse, Mia, and I haven't come to blows is a miracle.

The good news is that from the sounds of the arguing and even crying going on around the room, the other two teams haven't done much better.

I'm just cutting a thread from the sleeve of the jacket when Arthur calls, "Time! Step away from your mannequins."

I step back, not realizing that Jesse is kneeling behind me, and fall over him, almost stabbing us both with the scissors in my hand.

"Sheesh, Aria, are you trying to kill me?" he exclaims.

"No. It was an accident," I say. I stare straight into his eyes and raise my voice so everyone can hear what I say next: "But I could ask *you* the same question. Because you really *did* try to kill me."

A sudden hush comes over the room, and I hear the director ordering an additional cameraman over to cover us. But I keep my attention focused on Jesse. His Adam's apple rises and falls visibly as he swallows, and his face pales at least three shades under his makeup.

"Are you crazy? I don't know what you're talking about!"

"Really? You don't remember hiding my needle last week and putting another one on the table for me to find? One that you'd put an enchantment on that was supposed to kill me because I'm Brier Rose's daughter and you're Floriana Foxglove's grandson?"

"I didn't hide any needle—"

"Yes! You did!" Hugh shouts. "It's on tape. There's evidence!"

One of the cameramen nods, confirming Hugh's statement.

"Say it out loud," the director directs the cameraman on Camera 2. "Camera Four, get him doing it."

Camera 4 rushes over to film Camera 2, who says, "It's true. When I was reviewing the tape last week, I saw Jesse take Aria's needle when she went to get food. He put a different needle on her table. Then after she fainted, he took back the needle he loaned her. It's all there on the tape."

"That's not all," Mia says. The director holds up a hand so she'll wait to continue till there's a camera in her face. "I heard him talking to his grandma on the phone after the show. There was something on that needle that was supposed to have 'worked,' but it didn't, because Aria only fainted. Which means Jesse wanted something worse to happen to her."

"He wanted me to die, the same way his grandmother wanted my mother to die," I tell the camera. Looking down at Jesse, I say, "And all because she wasn't invited to a party."

That hits a deep-rooted Foxglove nerve. Jesse gives up all pretense of being innocent. Narrowing his eyes, he unveils his anger and lets it loose on me.

"It wasn't just any old party! It was *the* party. Everyone who was anyone in the entire kingdom was invited— except my grandmother. How would *you* feel?"

And that's when I realize the part I've been missing about the whole tale, the way it's always been told to me by my family—just how bad Floriana Foxglove must have felt. I knew she was mad—I mean, no one puts a death curse on an innocent baby just for kicks. No one ever talked about how hurt, sad, and rejected she must have felt to act out in such a terrible way.

"I'd feel awful. Just like your grandma did," I tell Jesse.

My admission surprises him, I can tell.

"Too right she did," he says. "The shame of it has nearly destroyed her."

"But do you seriously think my *mom* hasn't thought about that?" I ask Jesse. "Why do you think she started Enchanted Soirées? It's so that other people don't make mistakes like my grandparents and people don't get hurt like your grandma."

It's clear from Jesse's confused expression that this hasn't crossed his mind ever, not even for a second. He's been told the Foxglove tale his entire life, and just as Floriana Foxglove is the baddie in my mom's tale, my family plays the bad guy in theirs.

"I never . . . but . . ."

The anger seems to slowly leak out of him like air from a pricked balloon. What's left is . . . sadness.

I put out my hand and hope the cameras don't pick up that it's trembling.

"Need help getting up?"

At first I think he won't, that accepting my offer of a truce and understanding is too much to ask. But then he stretches out his arm and takes my hand. I pull him up, and he grasps my elbow with his other hand and gives it a squeeze. Everyone in the workroom claps—well, except for the camera guys and sound people, who are too busy making sure this whole drama is captured for posterity.

"Well, that was certainly *unexpected*," Arthur Dunn says. "Load your mannequins onto a hand truck and take them down to the studio. I'll meet you down there for judging."

After he leaves the room, the director yells, "CUT," and I'm relieved knowing the cameras are off.

"Wow!" Mia says. "That was freaking awesome!"

"Nice eavesdropping," Jesse tells her. "Now I know to watch myself around you."

"Yeah, next time you try to kill one of my friends, don't talk about it on the phone in a public place," Mia says.

The girl who I was afraid wanted to break my leg just called me a friend. I can't help smiling.

"Hey, teamwork, remember," I say, before they start fighting again.

I put my fist out. "Come on, Blue Team. We're in this together."

Mia rolls her eyes, but she puts her fist on top of mine, and Jesse reluctantly puts his on top of hers.

"Hey, if you three can work together, maybe there's hope for world peace," Iris says.

"Don't hold your breath," Lazlo says.

Sadly, I think Lazlo's right. We're just kids making clothes on a reality TV show about fashion. But maybe it starts with us. Maybe it's a little like what Mrs. Solano said about history and "herstory": If we had just paid more attention to one another's tales, the Foxgloves wouldn't have felt like they had to keep trying to kill us.

Mia, Jesse, and I load the Beast onto a hand truck and wheel him down to the studio for judging.

The Red Group chose Little Red Riding Hood, and they've made her look really funky and urban, like Little Red Riding Hoodie. She's got a black denim miniskirt with a rhinestone belt, and she's carrying a supermarket shopping basket.

The Green Group went for Cinderella, but instead of doing a ball gown, they've made her a uniform for Cinderella's Cleaning Service, like instead of being a slave to her stepmother and stepsisters, she's working for herself.

"Wow," I say to Mia and Jesse. "They had really good ideas."

"So did we," Mia says. "Don't doubt us."

She's right. The Beast looks like he'd be equally at home in a Jules Verne novel as in a fairy tale. He's a steampunk god. You'd never know by looking at him that one of our team members was trying to kill another one.

We're last down the runway, and hearing how much the judges like the other groups' designs just makes me even more nervous.

Finally it's our turn. We carry the Beast down the runway and set him in front of the judges. Mia describes our thoughts on the outfit, and my mouth is dry as I wait for the judges to comment. They just look at us, with strangely serious faces, for what seems like an eternity.

"It's not often—in fact, *never before* have we had an assassination attempt on a reality TV show," Mallory Anderson says. "So it's something we have to take very seriously."

Mia and I both look at Jesse, who has gone stone-faced, staring straight ahead, not looking at the cameras or the judges.

"While you did a terrific job of pulling together as a team and coming up with an innovative design, we—and the producers—feel that we can't ignore the attempt on Aria Thornbrier's life. Jesse, you're being cut from the show."

I exhale in a whoosh of air. I should be happy about this. This morning I would have wanted nothing more than for Jesse to be cut. But now . . .

"I understand," Jesse says in a quiet, steady voice. "I would do exactly the same thing in your position."

"It's not his fault," I protest. "He was told that tale his whole life!"

"But, Aria, I could have asked *why*, like you did. I could have tried to change things, like your mom does," Jesse says. "But I just believed the hateful things Grandma said and did what I was told."

He smiles ruefully. "Luckily, I'm not so great at spell craft, so you only fainted instead of died. For once, I'm glad to be a disappointment to my family."

"For what it's worth, Jesse, while you might not have great spell skills, you definitely show promise as a designer," Bailey Haberli tells him. "Even though you won't continue to share them here, I encourage you to stick with it."

Josie McGillicuddy seconds the motion. "Definitely. Learn from this, pick yourself up, and keep going."

"I will," Jesse says. "Thank you."

He looks at me.

"I'm sorry, Aria."

We hug each other, and then Mia joins in, and the director yells, "CUT!"

"Thanks," Jesse says to me. "I couldn't believe it when you stuck up for me like that, Aria. Especially after I gave you that needle."

"Neither could I, to tell you the truth," I admit. "But what's the point of carrying on a feud about something that happened before either of us were even born?"

"No point," Jesse agrees. "The only points I want to make from now on are fashion ones."

"By the way . . . you weren't a total failure at spell making," I tell him.

He perks up. "I wasn't?"

"Remember last week when I was talking to the judges and everything I said sounded like I was in a Shakespeare play?" I ask.

"I do!" Mia says. "So random."

"It was random because after I fainted, everything I said came out in Shakespeak. If you want to make your grandma feel better, tell her if we hadn't been able to find the cure, my mother might have killed me, it was driving her so nuts."

"No way!" Jesse exclaims. "I did the Spelle of the Elizabethan Tongue?"

"Yup. You wouldn't believe the gross stuff I had to drink to get cured. I should hate you for that alone!"

"I owe you a hot chocolate or a milk shake," Jesse says with that grin. "Something that tastes good."

Maybe I'll take him up on that someday.

If I can be 100 percent sure he won't put some enchantment on it.

Jesse goes off to say good-bye to everyone.

"That was something else," Mia says. "I had you pegged as a stuck-up princess, but I was wrong."

"I was wrong too," I admit. "I didn't want to work together today, but I'm glad we did."

We hug each other.

"See you next week," I say.

"Not if I see you first," she says, smiling over her shoulder as she walks away.

I go to find Grandma and Grandpa, who were watching from the audience. They're talking to Arthur Dunn, the director, and a man and a woman I haven't met before.

"Aria, my dear," Arthur Dunn says. "You really know how to bring it with the unexpected drama."

I'm not sure how to respond, because I don't know if they think it's a good or a bad thing.

"Um . . . ," I utter with exceptional articulateness, which I'm sure makes my grandparents swell with pride.

The man and the woman smile and nod.

"I'm Francine Cohen and this is Jeff Montalvo—we're the producers of *Teen Couture*," the lady says. "We were just discussing with King Thibault and Queen Althea what a great story line you've brought to the show."

"We think it'll help ratings if we promote that story line," Mr. Montalvo says. "Especially before this episode airs. We're going to approach Floriana Foxglove for an interview, and we want to get your parents on camera. We can run some great promos."

"Wait . . . what?" I sputter. "No."

They all stare at me like I'm speaking in tongues.

"What do you mean, 'no'?" Ms. Cohen asks.

"I mean, I don't want to promote the feud anymore. It's over."

"But it makes great television," Arthur Dunn explains. "Surely you can see that."

"I know it does. But it won't make great feelings for Jesse or his grandmother—or for Mom, or me."

"Don't you want to win this competition?" Mr. Montalvo asks. "This will up your profile with the viewers. It'll make you a household name."

"It'll be good publicity for Rose's business, too," Grandpa says.

I know what they're saying is true. But it still feels wrong.

Just then, Mom and Dad come bursting into the studio, followed by two policemen and several of the building security guards.

"Aria! You're alive!" Mom says, throwing her arms around me and bursting into tears.

It's good to know my mother's powers of observation are still as sharp as ever.

Dad engulfs us both in a princely hug. "Thank goodness. We were so worried."

"It's fine. It's all good," I tell them, happy that they are here.

Mr. Montalvo clears his throat. "Princess Rose, Prince Bernhard. I'm Jeff Montalvo, producer of *Teen Couture*, and this is my coproducer, Francine Cohen. We're delighted to meet you. We were just discussing making your story a bigger part of the show."

"It could be a great promotional opportunity for your party-planning business," Francine Cohen adds.

"Mom, Dad, can we talk for a minute?" I ask them. "In private?"

I see the producers exchange a glance, but then Ms. Cohen gestures to her assistant.

"Take them somewhere they can talk," she says, clearly not happy about this development.

The assistant leads us to a small, windowless room—I

think it might be a closet, but I don't care as long as I can talk to my parents without anyone listening. As soon as the door shuts, I tell Mom and Dad, "I need your advice."

"Of course, Aria," Dad says. "What's going on?"

I explain to them what happened. How all the clues were pointing to Jesse, and then when I accused him, he admitted it. But how I realized that every tale depends on who tells it—and that Jesse was brought up hearing Floriana Foxglove's side of the story.

"I can't totally blame him," I tell them. "I mean, he loves his family just the same way I love you."

"But you didn't try to kill him," Mom points out. "The only reason you're not dead is that he didn't inherit his family's gift for spell craft."

"He's happy about that," I point out. "He doesn't want to do spells. He wants to be a fashion designer." I square my shoulders and look at my parents defiantly. "Just like I do."

"How can you say that, especially now?" Mom says. "Can't you see—"

Dad puts a hand on her arm. "Rose. Let's hear Aria out."

"Jesse and I think this feud has gone on long enough. We want to be friends. But now the producers want to make a big deal about it and interview Mom, Grandpa and Grandma, and Floriana Foxglove. They want to play up the conflict angle because it would be good for ratings, even though Jesse and I are totally over it," I tell them. "But Grandpa says the publicity would be good for your business."

I look at Mom, holding my breath as I wait for her to tell me what she thinks I should do. She's staring off into the distance, and it seems like she's fighting an internal battle. I'm scared of what the outcome will be.

Dad puts his arm around her shoulders and gives her a supportive hug.

Finally Mom looks me in the eye.

"Forget about what's good for Enchanted Soirées," Mom says. "Let's talk about what's right for *you*."

I exhale, and the knot in my stomach begins to unravel.

"I want to move on," I tell her. "And if I win this competition, I want it to be because I'm a good designer, not because I'm Sleeping Beauty's daughter."

"That sounds perfectly reasonable," Mom says.

"Please don't think I'm not proud of you, Mom. I am. Seriously proud," I tell her.

"I know you are, Aria," Mom says. "But it's always nice to hear it."

"What if they won't let me stay on the show if I don't do it?" I ask.

"Then you have to make a choice," Dad tells me. "What's more important to you? Winning at any cost or doing the right thing?"

"I don't know," I wail. "I don't want to hurt anyone, but I want to win, too!"

"Sometimes you win in the long run by not hurting anyone in the short run," Mom says. "That's been the key to our success."

"We trust you to make the right decision, Aria," Dad says, hugging me.

Do I trust myself?

I feel like Mom when she was left all alone in the castle and was offered the spindle by Floriana Foxglove disguised as a crone. Should I take it or refuse?

"I don't know. Let's go back to the studio."

"Okay," Mom says. "Use your best judgment."

By the time I get back to the studio, I've made my decision.

"I'm sorry, but I can't do it," I say.

Frowns all around, especially on the faces of the producers. But Mom and Dad are smiling, so I'm pretty sure I've made the right choice.

"That will mean you can't—"

"Even if I get kicked off the show. I understand," I tell Ms. Cohen.

"Are you sure?" Grandma asks. "I thought being on this show was your dream."

"Being a designer is my dream," I tell her. "I can still do that without being on the show. Sure, I'll probably have to work harder at it, but at least I won't have to feel bad about myself."

I thank the producers for the opportunity and say good-bye to Arthur Dunn, who kisses my hand and says, "It won't be nearly as entertaining without you, dear."

I take one last look around the studio and say good-bye to my dream of winning *Teen Couture*, and then let my parents take me home.

Chapter Thirteen

THE *TEEN COUTURE* FINALE IS ON SUNDAY night, and Mom and Dad agree I can host a viewing party at our house. I've invited my friends from school and all of the other contestants who were cut. Mom even has Enchanted Soirées cater it, although with wings and lasagna and cupcakes instead of her fancier fare.

After weeks of competition, it's finally down to Hugh and Mia.

"Who do you want to win?" Nina asks.

"I don't know," I say. "I wish they could both win."

"You should still be in it," Matt grumbles. "I still can't believe you dropped out voluntarily."

"She followed her conscience," Sophie says. "I'm proud of her."

"Yeah," Rosie agrees. "Otherwise she might have ended up like my step-grandma, willing to do anything to win. Including trying to kill her own stepdaughter, not just once, but THREE TIMES!"

"I thought my neighborhood was tough, but Once Upon a Time sounds totally wack," Mia says.

"You don't even know the half of it," Dakota tells her.

"Yeah," Nina agrees. "The tales you guys hear are only a fraction of the *real* story."

The doorbell rings and I go to get it. Jesse stands there, holding a bouquet of daisies, roses, and foxgloves, and a bottle of sweet iced tea. Although we've stayed in touch, I haven't seen him in person since the day we both walked off the set of *Teen Couture*. I forgot how 100 percent adorable he is.

"I promised you something that tasted better than the cure for the Spelle of the Elizabethan Tongue," he says, handing me the iced tea. "And as for the flowers, well . . ." He blushes. "Those are for you."

"Thanks," I say, burying my nose in their scent. There's a question I want to ask him before we go in with the others. "How did it go . . . with your family?"

He gives me a wry grin. "Oh, that."

"Not so well?"

"Let's just say Grandma always said I was a blot on the family name, and apparently I've only proven her right—especially by coming here tonight and consorting with the enemy."

He glances down at the bottle of iced tea. "Don't worry, I'll try it first to make sure she didn't put a spell on it or anything."

I didn't even think about that. Apparently, I still haven't learned my lesson.

"Luckily, Mom is more understanding," Jesse continues. "She's had enough of the feud too. She told Grandma to stop messing around with spells and get therapy."

"Wow. I bet that went down well," I say.

"Grandma tried to turn Mom into a pillar of stone, but she accidentally got the cat. So now we have a petrified cat sculpture. Poor Fluffy."

I shouldn't laugh, but I do.

"I'm sorry," I say, trying to smother my giggles. "Poor Fluffy."

"It's okay. I went to the pound and adopted Cuddle-cakes," he says.

I stare at him, dumbfounded.

"But you *hated* Cuddlecakes," I point out.

"I wasn't feeling that great about the idea of killing you," he says, "so I took it out on Cuddlecakes. Okay, and I admit, I was annoyed because Cuddlecakes is the most stupid name for a dog *ever*. The first thing I did was change his name to Rocky."

The first thing I do when I get into the living room is introduce Jesse to my school friends. The second thing I do is announce that he adopted Cuddlecakes. "Except his name is Rocky now."

"No way!" Pez exclaims. "Does he still bite you?"

Jesse laughs. "No, if anything, he licks me to death. He's also taken the place of my alarm by barking at six in the morning to wake me up. Even on Saturday."

"And you haven't given him an enchanted bone yet?" Lazlo asks. "If a dog woke me up at six a.m. on a Saturday, I think I might."

"Nah. I just let him up on the bed and then he goes back to sleep."

Iris smiles. "See, more evidence that there's hope for world peace."

The first time Iris talked about peace, it sounded more like a fairy tale than any of the stories from Once Upon a Time. But if two families who have been feuding for over a century can give it up and learn to be friends, and Jesse can adopt Cuddlecakes—I mean, *Rocky*—then maybe someday we can make it happen.

The theme music for *Teen Couture* comes on, and I think about how excited I was to be on the show and how much I wanted to win.

Looking around the room, I feel like I've won anyway. Sure, I'm not going to get to have lunch with Seiyariyashi Tomaki, but both Mia and Hugh said they'd ask him anything I wanted to know. I would have loved to shadow him for a week, but Ms. Amara says she's going to help me find a summer internship with a design firm. Mom even said she might be able to help me get an internship at the Costume Institute at the Met. Now that I don't have to lie to follow my dreams and I have the support of my family, it feels like anything is possible.

Jesse comes over with two glasses and the bottle of iced tea. He pours some into each and then hands one to me.

"To a feud-free future," he says.

"A feud-free future full of fashion," I add.

We clink glasses.

I watch him take a drink first and wait to see what happens. When he doesn't die, fall asleep, turn into a newt or a petrified cute boy of stone, I laugh and drink some myself.

The iced tea is cool and sweet.

"This beats the cure for the Spelle of the Elizabethan Tongue hands down," I tell him.

He smiles.

Arthur Dunn's face fills the screen. "Welcome to the finale of *Teen Couture*. . . ."

We don't need Arthur to give us challenges. They're going to come whether he gives them to us or not. But I know that together all the people in this room can create the magic to overcome them—with or without a spell book.

Acknowledgments

THANK YOU TO THE WONDERFUL TEAM AT Simon & Schuster/Aladdin—it's so great to work with the wonderful Alyson Heller, publicist Aubrey Churchward, copy editor Kiffin Steurer, designer Laura Lyn DiSiena, and illustrator Angela Navarra for the gorgeous cover art.

Most fabulous agent, Jennifer Laughran, deserves a lifetime supply of Broadway tickets and the finest edible treats. I shall keep diligently writing books to ensure that she gets them.

I am a self-professed research geek, and indulging in my geeky passions is easier when you have interesting friends like Billy Serow, head of the Voice-Over Division at Abrams Artists Agency (NY), who was kind enough to explain the difference between a casting director and a casting agent, and Kyaiera Mistretta, Linda Urban, and @TheBestJasmine, who answered my callout for dog fashion questions on Twitter.

My fellow Swingers of Birches and Sisters of the Brass Necklace have my eternal gratitude for their smart, sassy suggestions and superlative sanity support. Y'all are the best, and that is no joke. Special props to Sarah Albee for her genius in suggesting the Shakespeak Solution.

To my beloved children, Amie and Josh, may your quest to pursue your life's passion go more smoothly than Aria's—and know that if it doesn't, Mom is here with love, hugs, chicken soup, and really terrible jokes.

Last, but never, ever least, thank you to my husband (!!), Hank Eskin, for booking the surprise room upgrade when we took our "prewedding honeymoon" while I was on deadline for this book, so that I could write on the balcony overlooking the ocean with the sound of a waterfall in the background. Twoo Wuv, indeed!